Centering KAOS

INTERNATIONAL BESTSELLING AUTHOR
HARLEY STONE

COPYRIGHT

Copyright © 2021 by Harley Stone
All rights reserved.
Published in the United States

This book contains material protected under International and Federal Copyright Laws and Treaties. Any unauthorized reprint or use of this material is prohibited. No part of this book may be reproduced or transmitted in any form or by any means, electronic or mechanical, including photocopying, recording, or by any information storage and retrieval system without express written permission from the authors, except in the case of brief quotations embodied in critical articles and reviews.

Centering Kaos is a work of fiction. Names, characters, places, and incidents are the products of the author's imagination and are used fictitiously. Any resemblance to actual events, locales, or persons, living or dead, is entirely coincidental.

❦ Created with Vellum

*For Jim and Deanna.
Thank you for your friendship and for challenging me to write Kaos's story!*

1

Tina

SHIFTING MY TWENTY-YEAR-OLD Mazda into park, I closed my eyes and leaned against the steering wheel. Rain drizzled outside, casting Seattle in its usual sloppy gray haze. Inside, I felt like I was suffocating, treading water as I fought for every breath.

I was familiar with the sensation, having almost drowned when I was six. Memories of that experience came flooding in, thinning the veil between past and present. It happened at the public pool, with a babysitter who was understandably focused on my four-year-old little sister. I couldn't really swim, but I was an expert at pretending to fit in with the hopes of being accepted. I'd clung to one of the older girls like a lifeline. The sweet, friendly older girl recognized my desperation for companionship and had taken me under her wing. She didn't ask if I'd taken lessons, and I didn't volunteer the information. When she and her friends drifted into the deep end, I didn't hesitate. I followed them right out of safety.

No longer able to touch the bottom and literally in over my head, I panicked. Down became up, left became right, and when I opened my mouth to call for help, water rushed in and choked off my cry. I kicked and flailed, coughing and desperate for air. Strength exhausted, lungs on fire, my vision blurred, and my ears rang. I blacked out.

I lived—obviously—but it still scares me that I was so desperate for acceptance I followed my new friend right off the deep end. I almost died that day, and, apparently, I hadn't learned a thing from it, or I wouldn't be here. Today's appointment wouldn't be necessary.

"Come home, honey. You know you belong with me. Don't make me kill you."

I was in over my head again. This time, I was drowning in the memory of my husband's fingers wrapped around my throat, squeezing the life out of me as he lovingly whispered the ultimatum into my ear. His words caressing my cheek as pain bit into my windpipe. Our relationship hadn't exactly been built on love, but I never expected it to turn so... lethal. Just thinking about that day made my skin feel too tight and my lungs too small. My heart tried to pound its way out of my chest as this new reality once again settled over me. This was our life now, and it was suffocating me. I struggled to suck down air as darkness clouded the corners of my peripheral...

"Are you taking me to Dad's?" a young male voice piped up from the backseat, reminding me I wasn't alone. And, I was Mom. Moms weren't allowed to have panic attacks or mental breakdowns. No matter how well-deserved and necessary they were.

Moms weren't allowed to give up and drown.

Determined to keep treading water, I forced my lungs to finally suck down a breath and unbuckled my seatbelt. It was time to rally. I'd need all the courage I could strum up to get out of the car, and I didn't have time to fall apart. Not today. "No. I told you, you can't go to Dad's anymore. He only gets supervised visits, and Melanie isn't available today."

Matt had already tried to abduct Dylan, but a brave young lady and her dog had intervened, saving my son and holding Matt until the authorities arrived. They should have locked up my estranged husband and thrown away the key, but he had no prior arrests and had played the concerned dad card like his stellar reputation was riding on the table. Ever since, Matt had stuck to our previous agreement and visits were arranged through Dylan's social worker, Melanie.

"That's stupid. Dad would never hurt me," Dylan grumbled.

Ice sliced through my chest. I used to think the same thing, but Matt had proven me wrong. I didn't know what that man was capable of anymore, and I wouldn't be underestimating him again. "You don't know that," I snapped without thinking.

Dylan's shattered expression filled my rearview mirror. I could have kicked myself for my thoughtlessness. I was the adult, and if I couldn't control my reactions, how could I expect my son to? As I watched, hurt bled from hazel eyes that mirrored mine, and his expression morphed into anger. "My dad is a good guy!" he shouted.

According to Dylan's psychologist, a healthy self-image depended on a child's views of their parents. I didn't want my son to ever even think about hitting a woman, so I'd opted out of telling him what his father had done to me. Matt said I fell down the stairs, and I didn't correct him. Dylan believed his dad hung the moon, and no matter how much it killed me, I refused to be the one who ripped that image apart. I'd kept my derogative comments about Matt to myself for months, but I could already tell this one little slip up was going to cost both me and Dylan greatly.

Beating my head against the steering wheel would only give me a headache, and more bruises, so instead, I apologized. "Of course he is. I'm sorry, Dylan, I was out of line."

They say apologizing makes you the bigger person. If that was true, I would no longer fit in this car. I'd taken the blame for so much over the years, spewing apologies to keep the peace. I didn't feel any bigger or more mature. All I felt was tired. Stifling a yawn with the back of my hand, exhaustion enveloped my body and seeped into every muscle and pore, all the way down to my fingernails and hair follicles. I couldn't even remember the last time I'd gotten eight uninterrupted hours of sleep, and I felt it. Hard. My tank was empty and I was riding on fumes. I didn't want to fight with my son. Heck, I didn't even want to fight with his father. I just wanted peace and quiet, maybe a vacation on an abandoned beach with a fruity adult drink in my hand. Unfortunately, war was on the horizon and I needed allies and resources, which was why I needed to make this appointment.

"Please get out of the car. We can't be late." I opened my door, praying Dylan would follow suit. I already felt like the world's worst mom and had no desire to carry him in, kicking and screaming. In his eyes, I was the bad guy who'd broken up our happy family and was keeping him from his perfect father. Since I couldn't set the record straight, at least not without revealing graphic details that would traumatize my child and send him to therapy for the rest of his life—not to mention breaking my agreement with Matt—all I could do was brace myself against the backlash.

By the time he unbuckled and climbed out of the car, I'd plastered a smile across my face. I held out my hand for him to take, but he only glared and shoved his hands into his front pockets. My heart stuttered, but my smile didn't falter. At eight, Dylan had gone through more than any child should. He was angry and hurt. His parents were battling, and his old life had become a casualty. I couldn't fault him for his emotions. The best I could do was to help him find a more appropriate way to channel them.

Maybe I'd buy him a punching bag.

Come to think of it, I could probably use one of those myself. Never again would I be one, that was for sure.

"It's this way," I said, stepping up on the sidewalk.

His footsteps splashed in the puddles behind me. No doubt there'd be mud on the back of my jeans and covering his. Whatever. I'd allow him this small rebellion if it made him feel better. I turned right, watching him out of the corner of my eye to make sure he followed. Dylan hadn't tried to run away, but he was becoming more sullen and withdrawn by the day. It was probably only a matter of time before he tried to make a run for it.

Great. That was one more worry to plague my nightmares.

Sliding a worn business card out of my pocket, I double checked the name and address of our destination. Having googled the non-profit organization at least a dozen times in the past six months, I had the information memorized. Still, touching the card had become a comfort, a reassurance that I hadn't exhausted all my options quite yet. Today, I would. Today, I would throw myself at their feet and beg for help if that's what it took. Shedding the last layers of my dignity with every step forward, I crossed the street and reached the office building with Dylan on my heels. I opened the door for him, and he scowled at me as he marched inside. Keeping my expression neutral—reacting to his hostility only seemed to increase it—I followed him in and gestured toward the elevator.

The ride up to the third floor took an eternity, giving me all the time in the world to second-guess myself for making this appointment. The down arrow called to me, promising a way out. All I had to do was push it, and we could walk right out of this building and pretend I'd never made the call. Of course, nothing would change, and I'd probably end up in an unmarked grave somewhere, but at least I'd have my pride.

Dear Lord, even my inner thoughts sounded ridiculous. The only thing that mattered was protecting Dylan and I had to stay alive for that. There was no pride in love, and I'd sacrifice every ounce of my ego to prevent my son from turning out like his father. I stuffed my hands in the pockets of my rain jacket, mirroring Dylan, and turned my back on the button.

"Will there be other kids there?" he asked.

"I don't know." I hoped not. Dylan used to be a friendly kid, but ever since my marital problems kicked into overdrive, he'd changed. Now he should be wearing a warning label announcing, 'Doesn't play well with others.' Even the sweet, thoughtful principal at his new school, Ms. Ruthchild, had declared him to be on her last nerve. Last week she said he was one detention away from receiving an out-of-school suspension.

Dylan crossed his arms and his scowl deepened. "This is gonna be boring. You should have taken me to Dad's."

The kid was relentless. I'd love to go one single day without fighting this battle. Heck, at this point I'd settle for a few hours of peace. I massaged my temples, trying to hold back the migraine I could feel coming on.

The elevator doors finally opened, releasing us onto the correct floor. I led Dylan down the hall until we found the door with the Ladies First logo etched into the glass. On the wall next to the door hung a welcome sign providing the business hours, a phone number, and instructions to "Please come inside." Knocking didn't seem necessary, but I rapped my knuckles against the door anyway as I turned the knob and let us in.

The waiting room was warm and inviting. Soft, gray walls held whimsical paintings. Cushy chairs and couches were situated around potted trees. Scattered coffee tables offered a variety of magazines. A massive tank full of colorful fish divided the space and provided calming sounds. The only thing missing from the room was people.

Ushering Dylan inside, I called out a tentative, "Hello?"

A man stepped out from the other side of the fish tank, and I nearly jumped out of my skin.

I'm not sure what startled me more. The fact that the first person to approach us in a women's crisis center was a man, or that said man was strikingly good looking... and big. Huge, even. Dark haired with dark eyes and a muscular build, he had to be well over six feet tall and outweighed me by more than a hundred pounds. I was average-sized, but I felt petite in his presence. His gaze roamed over my curves, and a smile tugged at the corners of his lips.

"Hello." His voice was a deep, rich baritone, making the word sound almost musical. My neck snagged his attention, and his eyes narrowed at the marks he saw there.

Reflexively, I felt the still tender skin and winced, knowing the bruises had faded to a hideous greenish-yellow color. This morning, I'd thought about covering them with a scarf or foundation, but I was done hiding and pretending. People needed to see the truth about my husband. Now, I regretted my rebellion. I hadn't banked on encountering a gorgeous giant in the waiting room. What was he even doing here?

"Sorry, I—" I took a step back, forcing Dylan behind me. "I think I have the wrong office."

"No." He shook his head and held up his hands soothingly. "You're fine. This is exactly where you need to be. I'm not... shit."

My eyebrows shot up at the curse word, and I glanced at Dylan, silently reminding the man that little ears were present.

His attention followed mine, and he winced. "Sorry. I... Uh..." Leaning back, he hollered over his shoulder, "Emily! Naomi! Your appointment's here!"

The frustrated, borderline panicked tone of his voice brought a brunette and a blonde running. Literally. As soon as they rounded the corner and saw me, they slowed to a fast walk and their faces lit up with wide, toothy smiles. The brunette wore a trendy navy dress under a blazer with matching pumps, looking polished and professional. The blonde sported a faded Harley Davidson T-shirt, worn jeans, and biker style boots. The two couldn't have been more different if they'd tried.

Coming to a stop between me and the man, the brunette extended her hand for me to shake. "You must be Tina." Her blue eyes were welcoming and friendly. "It's so nice to meet you. I'm Emily, and this is my friend, sister-in-law, and business partner, Naomi."

A little of the tension ebbed from my shoulders as we made

introductions, but I kept one eye on the big man. I couldn't help it; my gaze was drawn to him.

"Sorry if Kaos here startled you." Emily took a step back and patted the man's arm affectionately. "Our office manager is out sick today, so he's here to help."

"Chaos? Like disorder and confusion?" Who would name their kid such a thing?

"Kaos with a K," the man in question said with a grin.

"It's a road name, a nickname," Emily said. Then to Kaos, she added, "Thanks again. We owe you."

"Nonsense. Glad to do it." He took a tentative step forward and offered me his hand. "Sorry about the scare. It's nice to meet you, ma'am."

When we touched, a jolt of electricity zapped my hand. With a yelp, I yanked it back and rubbed it on my jeans.

"Sorry. Again." Kaos winced, shaking out his own hand. "The static in here is real."

Naomi and Emily shared a confused look at that, but Kaos plunged ahead.

"I would never... I'm not..." He looked to Emily for help, but she just patted his arm again.

"You're fine. We've got this," she said.

He let out a breath and backed up to the furthest corner of the waiting room where he sat on one of the cushy chairs. I got the feeling he was trying to make himself seem small and harmless, and I appreciated his effort. He'd done nothing to freak me out, not intentionally, and I needed to lock down my fear. I gave him an apologetic smile. He mirrored the gesture before dropping his gaze again.

Naomi took my arm and moved me further into the office. "I heard Lily gave you our card. She's such a sweet girl. Funny, too. I don't know if she mentioned it or not, but we work closely with a club of veterans who help us with things like security or moving furniture or whatever. Our husbands are both part of the club, as is

Kaos. As Emily pointed out, he's standing in for Jessica who manages our office, marketing, and social media. She's amazing, and usually sits with the children so we can chat privately."

Was she telling me this giant of a man would be sitting with Dylan? Wondering how my son would feel about that, I looked over my shoulder and found him staring at the man in open-mouthed curiosity.

"Dylan," I whispered.

He shook himself, and then gave me attitude. "What?"

I gestured him forward. "Come here."

He reluctantly wandered over, and I settled my hands on his shoulders.

Naomi's expression softened as she looked from Dylan to me. "Kaos wouldn't be here if I didn't trust him with my toddler. We screen all employees and volunteers, and so does the veteran's club. My brother only brings in standup men, and he holds them to a crazy high standard. To be around kids, there's additional training, and Kaos has completed it. We'll be one room away, and if your son feels at all uncomfortable, he can go right around that corner and find us in the first door on the right." She pointed in the direction.

Leaving my son with a strange man felt wrong, but if Kaos was a woman, I wouldn't hesitate. That revelation made me feel sexist, something I didn't care for at all. I'd researched Ladies First, thoroughly, and found nothing but glowing reviews. The organization had been founded less than a year ago, but they'd helped a lot of women in that time.

I needed to trust them to help me.

Emily knelt, coming eye-level with Dylan. "Hey, buddy. I'm Emily."

He didn't look impressed.

Resisting the urge to shake the attitude right out of him, I squeezed his shoulders until he looked up at me. Threatening him with my eyes, I whispered, "Manners."

He sighed but introduced himself.

Emily pointed to Kaos. "My friend there was a soldier in the Army. He also played professional hockey with the Sharks. Do you like hockey?"

I didn't have to see Dylan's face to feel his skepticism. "*He* was with the Sharks?"

A rumbling chuckle came from the far corner of the office.

Emily bit back a smile and nodded.

"Dylan plays the NHL video game," I said.

"Good." Emily smiled. "You two will have a lot to talk about. Kaos knows several guys in the league and I'm sure he has all kinds of fun stories to share. Will you sit out here with him while we talk to your mom?"

"For how long?" he asked.

"An hour, max."

He shrugged. "I guess. I don't have much of a choice, do I?"

My cheeks heated at his rudeness. We were going to have a serious conversation when we got home.

Kaos covered a chuckle with a cough. I checked him out again. He was a lot less intimidating sitting down, and the humor and kindness in his eyes put me at ease. Remarkably handsome with olive skin, a strong jaw, and dark eyes surrounded by a thick layer of lashes, he looked Mediterranean. Maybe Greek or Italian.

His gaze met mine, and the slightest hint of pity stared back at me, making my stomach roil. I would not fear this man, or any man for that matter. I would not cower and tie myself in knots to please anyone ever again. And I wouldn't put up with his pity, either. Squaring my shoulders, I squatted and turned Dylan to face me. "No, you don't have a choice. You'll be fine. If anything happens, you heard where to find me. Be good and listen to Kaos, okay?"

Dylan shrugged again. It wasn't exactly a commitment to behave, but it was as good as I was going to get.

"I got this," Kaos said with a reassuring smile. To my son, he added, "You any good at that NHL game?"

Dylan nodded and moseyed over in his general direction. "Maybe. What position did you play?"

"They'll be fine," Emily assured me, squeezing my shoulder. "Let's go chat."

Hoping she was right, I cast them one last glance and followed the women out of the room.

2

Kaos

I GREW UP in a big, Greek family where I learned to survive amongst a horde of savage siblings and cousins. We spent our younger years competing through a series of dares with little to no consideration for our personal health or the mental stability of our parents. There were several broken bones between the lot of us, but surprisingly enough, nobody died. Now, my cohorts were grown, most with little spawns of their own. Although I hadn't joined the growing list of family breeders, I prided myself on being everyone's favorite uncle, conquering family gatherings through gifts, horsey rides, wrestling matches, and video games.

The kids in my family didn't give two shits about my hockey career or military service. To them, I was a walking jungle gym to climb, tackle, and attempt to take down. I didn't dare show up without my bag of bribes, or they would rip my ass apart. The little curtain climbers kept me humble and always managed to put life into perspective, and I wouldn't change a damn thing about them.

Even outside of my family, children flocked to me. When I was with the Sharks, I'd been a staple in their Sharks & Parks program, delivering donated street hockey equipment to local youth organizations. I enjoyed riling up the kids to play and encouraging them to chase the shit out of their dreams. Our Q&A sessions were the best. I never knew what unfiltered insanity would come out of their mouths. The little bastards were brutally honest and unintentionally funny. Best fucking comedy shows I ever attended.

I volunteered to help the kids, but I'm sure I got a hell of a lot more out of the experience than they did.

The Dead Presidents, the veteran motorcycle club I'd joined after I got out of the military, ran an anti-bullying campaign at a couple local preschools. I'd taken the required classes and was on the waiting list to join them, but the guys who volunteered for that program didn't give up their spots easily. I'd probably have to shank someone to get a turn. Greedy motherfuckers.

Emily was a ball-busting attorney and the wife of my club president, Link. Naomi, a former Air Force helo pilot, was Link's sister, and the wife of Eagle, the club's secretary. Along with several other club ol' ladies, they'd founded Ladies First to offer support and resources to women who needed a hand getting out of bad situations and back on their feet. The ladies knew I wanted to work with kids, so when they called and asked me to sit with an eight-year-old who was struggling with his parents' separation, it was a no-brainer. But unlike the thousands of children I'd won over through my family and career, Dylan Parker didn't jump all over me or ask me to sign a poster or take a picture with him. Instead, he eyed me like I wasn't worth the oxygen in my lungs before taking his first verbal stab at me.

"They're gone. You can cut the crap now," he said, collapsing into the seat across from me.

I eyed him, wondering what his deal was. "Exactly what crap am I supposed to cut?"

"You might be able to fool them, but you can't fool me. I know you weren't in the NHL." He raised his chin, daring me to argue.

"Okay." I could pull out my phone, google myself, and prove it to him, but I kind of wanted to hear his reasoning. "How'd you come to that conclusion?"

"NHL players are... cool."

Ouch. That smarted. The kid sure didn't pull his punches. Hoping I didn't sound too wounded, I asked, "You don't think I'm cool?"

"You're a babysitter. You're babysitting me. That's not cool."

"Ah." I nodded, letting his reasoning sink in. He wasn't wrong, I was babysitting him, but if I was falling into the pit of Loserville, I was taking his little punk ass with me. "Doesn't that make you the baby I'm sitting? Babies aren't cool, either."

He stared at me like I was the biggest idiot on the planet. "No. I'm not a baby. When you watch someone else's kid, it's called babysitting. It doesn't have to be a baby, just a kid. Everyone knows that. You're not very smart, are you?"

I used to think I was, but this little bastard had me second guessing my IQ. I kind of wanted to brag about my BA in business but pulling out my college education seemed petty as fuck. We'd spent less than five minutes together, and my accolades hadn't earned me one ounce of his respect. I didn't know what scale Dylan was using, but he'd clearly taken my measure and found me wanting. The kid hadn't even given me a chance.

"You're kind of an asshole, aren't you?" I asked.

He gaped at me, looking a hell of a lot like he belonged in the fish tank in front of us. When his mouth closed again, it drew into a tight line and anger flared in his eyes. "You can't call me an asshole."

Impressed by how quickly his shock had morphed into indignation, I asked, "Why the hell not?"

"Because I'm a kid, and you're an adult. Adults aren't supposed to call kids names or cuss in front of us."

"Says who?" I asked.

My question seemed to frustrate him. "Everyone knows."

"Ah. The all-knowing everyone again. That seems to be your go-to answer for a lot of things. So, let me get this straight. I can't call you an asshole, but it's okay for you to behave like one?"

He rubbed his temple like I was giving him a headache. "Look, man, I don't make the rules."

I had to clamp my mouth closed to keep from laughing. As a kid, I'd made my mom massage her temples more times than I could count. I was guessing this little dude did the same. Poor Tina. I'd bet this shithead ran circles around her.

"Yeah, I don't think that's a rule, but I'll tell you what, you stop actin' like an asshole, and I won't call you one. Deal?" I asked.

He eyed me. "I'll think about it."

Damn, the kid was killing me. "Take your time." I sat back in my seat, resting my hands above my head. I kept my attention on the fish tank while Dylan's gaze burned a hole in my face.

We sat in silence for a few minutes as he studied me like he was trying to figure out all my weaknesses so he could use them against me. Finally, he announced, "You're big, but I don't think you're all that tough."

Another stab. The little bastard was really trying to cut me down to size. Probably so he could look me directly in the eye when he told me I wasn't shit. Ten minutes ago, my confidence was solid. Now, I was one more insult away from flexing on a pint-sized tormentor out of self-defense.

"You don't have many friends do you?" I asked.

He frowned, swinging his feet. Since they weren't long enough to hit the floor, they bounced off the chair's upholstery and kicked up until they were level with his knees. "I had lots of friends at my old school, but I don't get to see them anymore."

Well, shit. He and his mom must have moved recently. The kid was lonely and lashing out rather than dealing with his feelings. I couldn't blame him. If the fading bruises around his mom's pale neck were any indication, he was dealing with some heavy shit and probably didn't have anyone to talk to.

"Why don't you think I'm tough?" I asked, trying to keep him talking to see if he would open up.

"Those women are your bosses. Tough guys are in control. They don't put up with anyone's shit, and they don't let anyone tell them what to do. They're the bosses." He watched me, waiting for my reaction. Probably thought I'd jump on him for swearing, but I was far more bothered by his definition.

"Yeah?" I asked. "What gives a tough guy the right to tell other people what to do?"

"He's bigger and smarter. He knows what he's doing."

"Sounds more like a bully to me."

Dylan let out a dramatic sigh like *I* was the one making *him* want to pop antacids like candy. "You don't understand."

Oh, but I was afraid I did. "He's bigger, so he thinks he has the right to tell people who are smaller what to do. And when they don't comply, he beats them up. I don't care how you try to sugar coat it, that's a bully, Dylan."

He frowned. "Okay. If you're so smart, what do *you* think a tough guy is?"

I considered it for a moment, wanting to make this kid realize the ridiculousness of his point of view. A face popped into my mind, and I instantly had my answer. "When I was in the Army, I served with this guy by the name of Hirome Tagashi. He was so tough he earned the nickname Hero."

"Heroes aren't tough guys," Dylan announced.

"You don't like superheroes either?" I asked, unable to believe my ears. What the hell was wrong with the kid? How could anyone not like superheroes?

"No. Look at Spiderman. He risks his life for people all the time and what does he have to show for it? His uncle died. He's broke. His girl left him. He's a schmuck."

I stared at him. Kids didn't use words like "schmuck," which meant that some grown ass adult—probably some wannabe mobster—had planted that word in his head. Undoubtedly accompanied by a lot of nice guys finished last bullshit. "Who told you that?"

"My dad."

I wanted to point out that the biggest schmucks were those who were so weak they had to beat on women, but I bit off the words before they could pass my lips. I knew better than to talk shit about a kid's parents. That would only harm Dylan's self-image and turn him against me. Instead, I had to make him see the truth for himself.

"Look, Spiderman isn't real, but Hero is, and he's the toughest man I've ever met. He's not a big guy. Kinda short with a lean athletic build, but I'm tellin' ya, he's built out of vibranium wire, concentrated piss, and old-fashioned determination."

Dylan leveled a look at me. "Vibranium isn't real either."

"Nobody's proven that, but it doesn't matter. Hero was in Afghanistan when his vehicle hit an IED. That's like a hidden bomb on the side of the road. He was wounded on impact—got a leg full of shrapnel and dislocated his shoulder—and the vehicle fell under fire. That's what the enemy does, you know? They set up these traps and then they hide. When the vehicle hits the bomb, they start shooting. But Hero didn't cower in a corner like some pus..." I thought better of my word choice and censored myself. "Like some pansy. He slammed his shoulder back into its socket and managed to drag three of his unconscious teammates out of the vehicle to safety. All while the enemy was trying to shoot him."

Dylan stared at me with wide eyes, making me wonder if my story was a little too real and gory for a kid his age. I didn't want to traumatize him or give the kid nightmares. Before I could decide if I'd overshared, he snapped his mouth shut and skepticism clouded his eyes. "Yeah right. That kind of thing only happens in the movies."

I reached down and rolled up the left leg of my jeans, showing him the twelve-inch scar running down my shin before releasing my jeans and tugging up my T-shirt. Four jagged scars ran across my left side. I let him get a good look at them before dropping my shirt back into place and pointing out another thin, pale line that spanned from the bottom of my left ear to my shoulder.

"I was in that vehicle." One of five. Paulombo had been impaled during the crash and died instantly. Hero pulled me, Mayers, and Jacoby out of the wreckage and covered us until the rest of our convoy could surround us and return fire. Mayers didn't make it. He bled out during the flight to the hospital. But Jacoby and I owed our lives to Hero.

"Before that day, I would have considered myself tough. I can skate circles around most of the players I've met on the ice, and I've never lost a fight in my life. On or off the ice. But you know what? All my strength and training didn't mean a thing when my head bounced off the side of that rig and knocked me out." Still, I was one of the lucky ones, with only a concussion, a handful of scars, and no memory whatsoever of the attack. Jacoby had to have his left arm amputated and reconstructive surgery on his cheek, jaw, and nose. No amount of therapy seemed to help Hero stop reliving the attack in his nightmares. "Tough as I was, if it hadn't been for Hero, I would have died in that desert."

I pulled my phone out of my pocket and thumbed through pictures until I found the one I was looking for. In the photo, I stood beside an athletic Asian man who barely came to my shoulder and had a medal hanging around his neck and a haunted look in his eyes. A stocky white man stood on the other side, his arm a stump and his face still bandaged up from surgery. The three of us were dressed in service greens. Showing the screen to Dylan, I said, "See, that's me, Hero, and Jacoby. Hero saved us both."

Dylan's eyes practically bugged out of his head. "*He* saved *you*?"

I chuckled. "Sure did. That's one tough son-of-a-bitch right there." I watched the kid as my words sunk into his thick skull. I should have probably been watching my language, too, but sometimes it took a well-placed curse to really drive home a point, and I wanted to make sure this shit stuck with him.

"Any man can pick on those smaller than him, but real toughness... that comes from defending those who can't defend themselves. Being tough is about character and integrity. It's about who you are and how you react when the shit hits the fan."

Dylan's brow furrowed in thought. "With great power comes great responsibility," he quoted, and I got the feeling he was more of a Spiderman fan than he wanted to admit. There was hope for the kid yet.

"Fuckin' A, man." I'd said enough on the matter and didn't care to keep preaching. Besides, my street cred couldn't hold up against being called uncool again. Switching gears, I sought out our common ground. "But enough about all that. Which console do you play NHL on?"

He sat a little straighter and a proud smile tugged at his lips. "PS 5."

"Wow. Your mom found you a PS 5?" I'd been trying to get one for my nieces and nephews for a while, but the damn things were sold out everywhere. The only way to get one was through a scalper who bought them at retail and resold them at hiked up prices. During my hockey days, I'd invested well and could comfortably live out the rest of my life without ever working again. I had the dough, but I refused to buy from scalpers out of principle. Those fuckers were ruining the entire system, making it so only the rich had access to new tech.

"Nope. Not Mom. My dad got it for me. He works for a software company, and he can get anything."

And I'd bet he paid a pretty penny for it, too. Emily and Naomi hadn't told me much about Dylan's situation. I knew he and his mom had moved out about seven months ago, and that his dad had physically abused his mom a few times. The man was apparently trying to buy his son's love with expensive game consoles and sounded like a real piece of shit to me.

"What's your favorite team to play?" I asked.

"The Canucks," Dylan replied without hesitation.

"Ah. They have some standup guys."

His eyes widened. "You really know them?"

I shrugged. "Not some of the newer guys, but the older fellas, yeah."

Now I had his full attention, so I spent the rest of the time dropping names and sharing stories, shamelessly earning the kid's respect through the players I'd had the privilege of getting to know. By the time the ladies emerged from their appointment, I was well on my way to winning him over. It had been at least a half hour since he'd taken a stab at me, and he actually seemed disappointed when his mom appeared and asked if he was ready to leave.

I might have started out as an uncool babysitter, but hell if I didn't redeem myself.

Dylan looked at me and hesitated like he wasn't sure about the protocol for our goodbye. I had no such reservations and held out a hand for him to shake, man to man.

"It was good to hang out with you, my man," I said.

"You too, Kaos." Dylan's handshake was firm, and his smile seemed genuine. He'd been a hard nut to crack, but I always did enjoy a good challenge.

His mom's pensive stare drew my attention. Tina was a natural beauty with light brown hair, big hazel eyes, and plump lips. She was only about five and a half feet tall, but she had the kind of curves that made a man want to grab a handful and hold on tight. Dressed casually with minimal makeup, she had an intriguing girl-next-door look about her. If I met her in a bar, I'd try my damnedest to take her home. Knowing she came with a hell of a lot of baggage didn't dim her appeal one bit, but she was a mom, and that kept my ass in line and my tone respectful.

"You've got a good kid here," I said, standing.

Her eyebrows rose in question as she looked from me to Dylan like she was waiting for the other shoe to drop. When she realized I had nothing more to say, her guard dropped, and she smiled. She had a nice smile. It raised her cheeks and added life to her tired eyes, taking her from pretty to stunning. "Thank you."

Dylan looked up at me and opened his mouth as if to say something, but instead, he looked away. The kid wanted something but didn't know how to ask. The hour I'd spent with him made me think about a motivational poster I'd seen hanging on the office wall of the administrator for the Sharks & Parks program. *'Every kid is one caring adult away from being a success story.'* I didn't know if the Josh Shipp quote held water, but I was willing to give it a try.

Dylan wasn't a bad kid.

Sure, he was a bit of a bully and kind of a smartass, but I liked him. He reminded me of myself at that age. My parents would get a kick out of him for sure. Especially since they didn't have to raise him.

When I'd acted like a little shit, my coaches, teachers, and family cared enough to knock some sense into me, but who did Dylan have? A dad who beat the shit out of his mom and tried to buy his love?

Making a split-second decision I'd probably regret later, I turned to face Dylan. "You know, if you ever want to learn how to play hockey, I'll teach you."

His gaze shot up to meet mine. "Really?" He searched my face, and I got the impression he was waiting for some kind of condition or requirement.

I only had one. "As long as it's okay with your mom."

"Can I, Mom?" Dylan asked, his tone hopeful.

Tina frowned. "That's probably not a good idea." To me, she added, "Dylan has been having some behavioral issues, and we don't really have the money—"

I held up a hand, cutting her off. "No charge." I didn't need the money, and there was no way in hell I'd accept payment from a single mom.

She stiffened and distrust clouded her eyes. "Thanks, but I don't think so."

"But Mo-om," Dylan whined.

"Come on. We need to get going."

Clearly people didn't go out of their way to help this woman. I realized how I must have sounded—a grown ass man offering to coach her son for free—and shook my head. "Wait. I'm screwin' this all up."

Her eyebrows arched in question.

"Look, I'm not a creep or anything. I was a lot like Dylan, so I understand what he's going through. Went through a rough patch myself around his age. Got in so many fights my parents were one suspension away from sending me to military school. Thankfully, a teacher stepped in and sparked my interest in the game. Gave me something else to hit." Mr. Dens had handed me a hockey stick and dropped a puck on the ice, instructing me to swing as hard as I could. Yeah, he'd given me something else to hit, but not before I landed on my ass enough times to take the steam out of my sails.

Tina watched me intently. She wasn't checking me out, more like interrogating me with her eyes. Her attention was uncomfortable, like when a cop follows you and you know you're not doing anything wrong, but you still feel nervous as hell. I was telling the truth and trying to help her kid out, but her scrutiny made me feel like I was about to get a ticket for some traffic rule I didn't even know about.

"Changed the whole course of my life," I said. It did, too. I owed Mr. Dens more than I could ever repay. If he hadn't put me on the ice, I had no idea where I'd be today. Nowhere good, for sure. "Team sports are… imperative for children. Can't say enough about the benefits, but you should do your own research on the topic. It's crazy all the ways bein' part of a team can help a kid." And I really wished I could remember some of those ways, but Tina's intense, hazel eyes were locked on me, making it difficult to think. I needed to wrap this up and get out of her headlights before I started sweating and stammering. "Anyway, I wasn't a bad kid. I just needed a little direction. Kinda like Dylan here."

"Yeah, I just need some direction," Dylan parroted, still watching his mom hopefully.

Tina gave her son a small smile. She still didn't look sold, but I was done with my spiel. If she didn't want my help, I wouldn't push.

"No need to answer today." I walked over to the front desk and scribbled my name and number down on a Post-It. "Just think about it and let me know. No pressure. The veteran group I'm a part of... we like to help people out. Even if you and Dylan don't decide to pursue hockey lessons, you should keep this number. If you ever get into trouble or need help, just call and we'll be there."

I handed her my info. She gave me one more intense stare down before pocketing the Post-It with a nod. "Thank you." Her eyes were glassy when she turned to face the ladies. "Thank you all."

"Of course," Naomi said. She and Emily had watched our exchange quietly.

"We're happy to help," Emily added.

Tina gave me one last lingering glance before shooing her son out the door. The second they were gone, Emily and Naomi spun around to face me. Their smiles had vanished. Emily's face was pale, and she rested a hand on her stomach like she was about to puke.

Gritting out a curse, Naomi slapped the empty wooden coat rack, sending it crashing to the floor.

Feeling completely out of the loop, I asked, "So... what'd I miss?"

3

Kaos

"WHAT THE FUCK is that?" I asked, studying the photograph Emily slapped down on the table. We were in the conference room she and Naomi used for meetings. She had a file open in front of her, and her face was an unreadable mask as she followed my gaze. That had to be her lawyer face.

"That is the kind of thing I'd hoped to avoid by switching my focus from criminal to family law," Emily replied.

We both stared at an image of a naked woman tied up with rope, gagged, and covered in black, blue, and purple bruises. The exposure was a little dark, but what I could see of her face, hair color, and body shape, the woman looked mighty fucking familiar. My blood pressure spiked as bile rose up in the back of my throat. "Tell me that's not Tina."

Emily eyed me curiously, seemingly surprised by what she'd heard in my voice. That made two of us. "It's not her. It's the reason she left her husband. Well, there were many reasons, but this was the catalyst."

She wasn't making any sense.

Frustrated, I looked to Naomi. "If that's not Tina, who is it?"

Naomi's mouth was set in a hard line, and there was murder in her eyes. "A hooker. Tina's bastard of an ex apparently pays this woman so he can smack her around whenever his anger gets the best of him. Keeps him from beating the shit out of his wife." Sarcasm and venom dripped from her words. "He's so considerate. A real fuckin' giver."

"I don't understand." I struggled to make sense of the bits and pieces they were giving me. "He *does* beat on Tina. Or someone does, at least. I saw the bruises on her neck."

"Now he does," Emily replied. "About seven months ago, she was cleaning out the garage and found a box of these pictures stashed away. She said there had to be at least a couple dozen of them. Apparently, Matt likes to keep trophies of his abuse."

"The bastard caught Tina looking through the box and came clean," Naomi spat. "The fucker called it a kink. Made Tina feel like she was shaming him for getting upset about it. He even tried to lay the blame on her, saying she should be taking care of his twisted-ass needs. Like being an abusive sadist is some physical requirement and he's a saint for paying a hooker so he could spare his wife. Give me five minutes with that cocksucker and I'd take care of his fucking needs, all right. I'd even pay his ass for the experience."

Emily raised her eyebrows at Naomi.

Naomi shrugged. "Well, I'd slip a hundred-dollar bill into his coffin."

I liked Naomi. She made sense to me. "I want in on that action," I muttered. Now, I studied the photo with renewed purpose, mapping out every bruise on that woman. I fully intended to repay each one to her abuser.

An inferno blazed inside me.

I've always had an explosive temper. When I was a child, my folks would go out with my aunts and uncles, leaving all of us kids together in one house. They only had two rules: no deaths and no breaking shit. You'd think they'd be easy rules to follow, but we were a rowdy bunch, with more energy than brain cells. Once, a couple of my cousins were wrestling and knocked over a table lamp, shattering it. I was on the other side of the table, and both those assholes tried to pin the blame on me.

To be fair, whenever something broke, I was usually guilty, but this time, I didn't do it. Determined to make them eat their bullshit accusations, I attacked. The lot of us were rolling around on the floor throwing punches when my three older brothers intervened. They tackled me and trapped me in the coat closet. They intended to let me out as soon as I chilled out, but being locked up for a crime I hadn't committed flipped a switch inside of me. I couldn't turn it off. The longer I stayed locked up, the harder I raged.

By the time our parents returned, I'd torn the shit out of that closet.

I was so riled up the adults had to keep me restrained. They tried to unravel the truth about what had happened, but in the end, the facts didn't matter. We all got our asses beat and were sent to bed. After that, my cousins slept with one eye open every time they stayed the night. The fuckers knew I'd be gunning for them, and I was. My revenge came after months of plotting and preparing. With a low voltage electric wire slipped into our swimming pool at the perfect time, I taught both my cousins and my brothers a lesson about fucking with me.

My oldest brother, Gregory, still complained about occasional numbness in his fingers and toes.

To be honest, it was a wonder any of us survived childhood.

So yeah, I knew what it was like to lose my temper. But no matter how pissed I got, I'd never laid a hand on a woman in anger. Not even close.

Naomi turned on me, her expression reflecting the fury I felt. "You want to know the most fucked up part of this whole thing?" Before I could respond, she answered her own question. "If Matt hadn't caught Tina looking at those pictures, she never would have said a word. Her husband would still be out there beating the shit out of his paid side piece and coming home to her like he was a respectable family man."

Emily looked worried, but I couldn't tell if her concern was for Tina or Naomi. "We don't know that for sure."

Naomi threw her hands up. "We sure as hell do!"

"Is Tina a doormat?" I asked. She hadn't seemed like a pushover when she was staring into my soul, trying to figure out why I was so interested in her son. She'd protected Dylan, pushing back about letting me coach him. "Didn't seem that way to me."

"No, she's…" Emily snapped her mouth closed.

"It's complicated," Naomi added.

"And that's not our story to tell, Kaos. We're only sharing case information with you because we have a plan, and we need your help." Emily's gaze turned pleading. "Will you help us?"

"You don't even have to ask." They couldn't take me off this case if they tried. I was fully roused now. I had questions and concerns and was ready and willing to take down the bastard. Rolling my head from side to side, I worked out the kinks like I used to before I took the ice. "Just tell me what I need to do."

Emily removed a packet from her file and set it on the table. "Matt Parker is dangerous."

My gaze slid back to the photo. "Obviously. How did she get the marks around her neck?"

Naomi stopped pacing long enough to answer. "Fucker jumped her outside of her workplace. Threatened to kill her if she doesn't come back to him."

"Why isn't he in jail?" I asked.

"Oh, he's an upstanding citizen," Naomi sneered. "A smart one, too. No witnesses, no evidence other than the bruises they can't pin on him, and he had an alibi. The cops think it was some random attacker who was interrupted before he could rape her."

"But that photo," I argued. "You said Matt has a box of them."

Emily frowned. "Tina pocketed the one before she moved out, but there's nothing to tie it to Matt."

"But you said the woman's a prostitute. What if we find her?"

"It's pointless to even look for her. She won't talk," Emily replied. "Trust me. No local prostitute would dream of taking the stand against her john. Prostitution is still illegal here, and it'd be the end of her career, if not her life."

"There has to be a way to nail his ass," I said, not bothering to hide my disgust.

"Not for that," Emily said, picking up the picture and tucking it back into her file. "People are still innocent until proven guilty, and without evidence or witnesses we have no case."

Naomi leaned over Emily's shoulder. "I feel for the hooker, I really do, but we can't forget what Matt did to our girl." Plucking another photo from the file, she handed it to me.

Tina. This one was her; I would bet my life on it. One eye was swollen shut, but the other was unmistakable. Her lip was busted, and a fist-sized bruise covered the right side of her jaw. Naomi added a second photo to the first. This one was a torso shot. Tina wore a sports bra and boy shorts, but almost every inch of her exposed skin was covered in bruises.

"Holy shit," I swore.

"Yeah. That's what he did when he caught her with her hand in that box of photos." Naomi picked up another picture, studied it, and then flipped it around to show me. A blond-haired, blue-eyed man wearing a business suit. He looked like the average corporate Joe, medium build, friendly smile. The man even had a fucking dimple on full display. "Meet Matt. He's got the predator mullet going on. Hard-working family man on top, abusive sexual deviant just beneath the skin."

That old pre-hockey rage reared its ugly head. Once again, I felt like an enraged kid, ready to destroy walls, shred clothes, and bust heads. This time, a harmless prank wouldn't be enough to sooth my beast.

I wanted Matt Parker's blood.

Through my haze of fury, something nagged at the back of my mind. This was the proof she needed, which could only mean one thing. "She didn't go to the cops."

It wasn't a question, but Naomi shook her head anyway.

"They made a deal." Emily gathered up the photos and returned them to her file. "A good mother will always sacrifice herself for her child, and Tina loves her son. She gave Matt an ultimatum. She promised not to press charges as long as he let them move out without a fight and agreed to supervised visits with Dylan."

"So, he beat the shit out of her and got away with it. That's some serious bullshit."

"She was smart," Emily countered. "With no priors or witnesses, it's her word against his. She would have to file charges within seventy-two hours of his arrest. He might have gotten a full fifteen days in jail, but I doubt it. She had no money of her own, no one to really help her."

"She had limited plays available, and the game was rigged to let him win," Naomi said. "Tina moved in with her sister, and as soon as her bruises were gone, that bastard went back on his word and tried to kidnap Dylan. That's how she got our card. Lily and her dog were in the park that day. They attacked Matt and stopped him from getting away with the boy. Unfortunately, he knew just what to say to make it look like a misunderstanding between parents. The cops didn't even book him."

"So, he still has no fuckin' record," I growled, amazed at how much the asshole had gotten away with.

"Exactly." Emily nodded. "He laid low until last week when Tina told him she wanted a divorce. He wouldn't even discuss it. The next day, he caught her in the parking garage outside of her workplace and left her that colorful scarf of bruises."

Matthew Parker needed someone to rip his larynx out through his asshole, and I was just the man for the job. Bet the bastard would have a hard time talking his way out of charges then.

"Do we need to call in someone else?" Emily asked.

"What? No!" I couldn't even believe she'd asked such a thing. I was in. I was so fucking in, I could already feel my hands wrapped around that little peckerhead's throat, ready to give him a taste of his own medicine. My face felt hot, and my heart pounded against my chest. Never in my life had I wanted anything as badly as I wanted to fuck this motherfucker up, which—as I watched the growing concern on Emily's face—I realized might be the problem. "No. I've got this."

"You sure?" Naomi asked. "Because steam is coming out your ears and your eyes are starting to glow. It's cool that you care and want justice as bad as we do, but we can't let you out on the street like this. You need to get your game face on."

Emily nodded, jabbing me with a finger. "If you lose your temper and blow your cover, we'll miss out on this opportunity. We have a plan. It's a good one, and I will bring the wrath of God down on you if your temper screws it up. If you end up in jail and Matt walks free, you and I are gonna have a problem."

"Maybe we overshared," Naomi said to Emily, talking about me like I wasn't even there and acting like she wasn't just throwing down the coat rack and making death threats. "Next time, we should stick to the task we need performed and not share the why."

Emily eyed me. "Yeah, but I wanted him to know what he's dealing with. Matt's manipulative. He'll try to talk his way out of it. And when he can't, he'll come after Tina. She'll need our protection. I have a feeling about this one, and my senses are telling me she's in more trouble than she can imagine. Nobody ever believes their husband is capable of murdering them. Especially not a husband who looks like Matt." She pointed at his picture. "He's wearing a pocket protector, for crying out loud."

Naomi frowned. "Maybe we should call in Bull."

They wanted to replace me. I needed to get myself under

control, because there was no way they were yanking me from this case. They didn't need my fists or my fury. No, there were other ways to knock a motherfucker off his feet. I could do it their way. Matt needed a missile of karma up his ass, and when the smoke cleared, I wanted to be standing over his corpse, holding the launch codes. Determined to bottle my rage, I filled my lungs with air, held my breath while I counted to ten, and then blew out my anger. Feeling marginally better, I repeated the process. Both ladies watched in fascination as I felt the excess blood drain from my face. Unclenching my fists and rolling the tension out of my shoulders, I said, "Okay. I'm good now."

"Neat trick," Naomi said with a smile.

"Thanks. Kept me out of the sin bin a time or two."

"The sin bin?" Emily asked.

"Hockey slang for the penalty box," Naomi provided. "Our boy here played center, which meant he was needed on the ice making plays. He had to keep his temper in check, or his coach would kick his ass."

She knew about me. Feeling played, I arched an eyebrow. "Didn't know you were a fan."

Her smile widened. "There are a lot of capable veterans in the Dead Presidents, but we make sure we get the right man for the job. Now that your inner hockey beast is contained, I think you got this, Kaos. Actually, I know you do." She looked pointedly at the prospect patch on my cut. "This is your chance to prove yourself, and you won't let us down."

Her faith in me was humbling and welcome as she reminded me of what was at stake. One of my favorite things about the Dead Presidents was that everyone started at the bottom. They were unimpressed with the accomplishments of my past, requiring me to perform in the present. The ladies were giving me a shot to do just that, and Naomi was right. I wouldn't fuck it up.

But this was about more than a patch on my cut.

This was about helping a terrified single mom and her wayward son get out from under the thumb of a narcissistic son-of-a-bitch. I'd keep my cool to help Tina and Dylan.

Rolling my shoulders again, I cracked my neck. "All right. What's the plan to bring this shitstain down?"

Emily smiled and steepled her fingertips. "Well, it starts with pizza."

4

Kaos

PIZZA.
When Emily first muttered the word, I thought it was a metaphor for something, but no, I was delivering pizza.

Neither my bike nor my Escalade made for a believable food delivery vehicle, so I borrowed Naomi's Subaru. As I picked up the order, I couldn't help but chuckle at my assignment. Since life before the service had consisted of nothing but school and hockey, I'd never actually had a job. Now, my volunteer work had me pretending to be gainfully employed at Pietro's Pizzeria. If my old hockey buddies could see me now, I'd never hear the end of it.

Well, until they saw that picture of Tina all covered in bruises with a black eye and a split lip. Then they'd gladly slip into the same company T-shirt I was wearing and join me on this little adventure. When we finished with Matt, Tina wouldn't even need a divorce.

Matt lived in an upscale neighborhood in Duvall, a suburb of Seattle. As I navigated in his direction, I decided being a pizza delivery man wouldn't be so bad. It'd get me out of the house and keep me busy, enabling me to discover unfamiliar neighborhoods and meet new people. If I ended up losing my shit, botching this job and killing the motherfucker, maybe I'd give it a try.

After I carefully disposed of his body, of course.

The navigation app led me to a perfect family home with two executive-level vehicles parked in the driveway and another at the curb. Just as Tina had said, Matt was hosting himself a little get-together to watch basketball. She knew about the party because during their last supervised visit, Matt had invited Dylan. He knew damn well the boy wouldn't be allowed to attend, and only did it to stir up shit with Tina.

I couldn't wait to ruin the bastard's day.

Parking behind the car at the curb, I cut the ignition and tried to make sense of the house. I'd pictured something dark and ominous, but the two-story craftsman was painted a cheerful blue. In my mind, there had been bars on the windows, but these windows were flanked by white shutters. A matching picket fence lined the professionally cut and edged lawn. Colorful flowers lined the walkway, and there wasn't a weed in sight. A welcome sign even hung over the doorbell, and the mat beneath it celebrated spring.

This was the home Matt had shared with his wife and child.

He had stashed pictures of his abused hooker here.

The bastard had beaten the shit out of his wife just on the other side of that door.

It should have looked like a prison.

Boxes in hand, I headed up the driveway. The front window was open, allowing me to hear the game buzzer followed by indecipherable mutterings of the announcer. Cheers responded. The game was in full swing, and Matt and his buddies were into it. Good. Their distraction would make my job all that much easier.

Keeping the paperwork Emily had given me out of sight between the two pizza boxes, I situated the receipt on top of the box and checked the pen I'd snagged from the pizzeria. When it drew a black line on the box, I knew I was good to go and rang the doorbell.

I'd been expecting the man in the photo to answer, so the stout balding man who opened the door threw me off. Before I could say anything, his gaze zeroed in on the boxes in my hand, and he shouted, "Who ordered pizza?"

He swung the door wider, revealing a living room with two brown leather sofas and a matching recliner. The place was crowded with men. Heads turned toward us, and I scanned the faces finding no sign of Matt.

"Who cares? Just grab 'em and shut the door," someone said. "The light's reflecting on the TV."

The stout balding man reached for the pizzas, but I stepped back.

"Sorry, I have a message for a Matt Parker and need a signature." Nobody else would do. If I didn't get Matt's John Hancock, today would be a flop. I'd be burned, and the ladies would have to come up with another plan that didn't involve me. I had not come this far to be cut out now.

Someone shouted for Matt.

The blond haired, blue-eyed, dimpled pretty-boy came around the corner and smiled at me.

Much like his house, Matt was a deception. He reminded me of a kid I'd once played hockey with. The motherfucker would smile and wave at the crowd with one hand while he cup checked his opponent with the other. I'd never had much use for people who took cheap shots, and I still carried around a bit of PTSD from those fists or sticks to the groin. Everything about Matt Parker made me want to drop the boxes and rearrange his pretty face. Making the outside of him look as repulsive as the inside would be hella satisfying.

But that wasn't the job.

So, I plastered a smile on my face and forced myself to ask, "Matt Parker?"

He nodded. "Yeah, but I didn't order any pizza. There must be some sort of mistake."

"No mistake. The order was placed by a..." pretending to read the ticket, I said, "Bill Orwell. He wants you to know he's sorry he can't make it to your party, but wanted to send over a couple pies as a thank you for the invite."

"You gotta be fuckin' kidding me." A dark-haired man stood from one of the couches and glared in our general direction. "I know you're after that raise, Parker, but inviting the boss...? That's low, bro. Even for you."

"Got something on your nose there, Parker," someone else added. "Should probably shove that beak further up Orwell's ass to wipe it off."

"Oh, come on, you all know I didn't invite Orwell," Matt argued, turning to face the group. "Which one of you assholes set me up?"

Tina said mentioning the boss would stir up a hornet's nest, and it sure did. I was only hoping Matt didn't refuse the pies to appease his boys. Doing my best to play the role of a disinterested minimum wage employee, I said, "Look, man, they're paid for, and I have other deliveries to make. Eat 'em, toss 'em out, give 'em away, I don't care. I just need your signature on this line so I can bounce." I angled the boxes toward him and held out the pen.

"If that old bastard ever shows up to watch a game with us, I'm out," someone announced.

"Yeah, me, too." Matt said, taking the pen from me. "Next game, you all better bring your own beer, because I'm not supplying if you're gonna treat me like this."

He signed the receipt, and I gave myself a mental fist bump as I pocketed the paper and slid the packet of paperwork out from its hiding spot between the boxes. I slapped it on top and passed everything to Matt.

He instinctually accepted the package even as confusion contorted his face. "What the hell is this?"

I gave him a shit-eating grin and took a big step back, preparing to make my escape. "Divorce papers. Congrats, motherfucker, you've been served."

The shock that registered across his features was some next level shit. Pleased, I turned to leave.

"Divorce...? Served? Wait. Tina... Have you seen my wife? Where is she?"

He sounded genuinely concerned. No, more like heartbroken and desperate. Had I not seen the proof of his brutality, I would have second-guessed the situation. Now understanding why Emily and Naomi had shared the photos with me, I ignored him and kept walking.

"Please, you have to help me. She's... she's messed up in the head. I'm worried about her, man. If you have any idea where she is... I only want to get her some help, you know?"

"I'm sure you do," I said over my shoulder, not buying his lies for a second. "I'm sure you'd like to beat some help right into her, asshole."

I almost made it to the Subaru before he shouted at me to wait. I'd had enough of his bullshit, so I gave him what he wanted. I stopped and turned to face him. "What?"

"Have you seen her? Is she okay?"

After what he'd done, he had no right to ask. And that forced concern in his eyes... it only made me want to knock his ass out. "She's still sporting the bruises from when you tried to strangle her, but she's good. Way to show concern about your victim. It's really fuckin' believable." I gave him two thumbs up like the smartass I was.

His expression fell. "That wasn't me. I didn't lay a hand on her. She has some mental problems and she... Man, I think she's self-harming. She's a danger to herself and our son."

I was onto him, but that clearly didn't mean a damn thing. The bastard was still trying to convince me. And he was good... really fucking good. I wondered if he believed himself. Goddamn pathological liar. He might be able to gaslight the authorities, but his sad expression and business-casual khakis and button down on a Sunday didn't fool me. I didn't trust men who weren't even comfortable enough to dress down on a weekend. "Sure. She strangled herself. Seems perfectly legit. For the record, I'm not interested in any Arizona ocean front property you have to sell, either."

"How dare you." He glanced behind him, but we didn't have a crowd. Everyone was more interested in the game than they were the delivery man. Matt straightened his shoulders—so he no longer looked like a kicked puppy—but kept up his game. "I would never hurt my wife. I just want her back safe."

I chuckled, letting a little of my anger seep into the sound. "Yeah? Well, I'm pretty sure back with you is the most dangerous place she can be. Stay away from her if you know what's good for you."

Emboldened by my jab, he leaned forward. "That a threat?" Taking in my worn jeans, T-shirt, and boots, he turned his nose up at me like I wasn't shit. I hadn't bought his innocent routine, so now the bastard was trying to put me in my place. "By a delivery boy? Maybe you should stay in your lane so you don't get hurt."

Thought his nice house and high-paying job made him a bigger man, did he? Didn't matter. I knew who the fuck I was. Let him underestimate me; I enjoyed it. One phone call, and my financial advisor could liquefy enough assets to buy Matt's company and send him packing if I really wanted to.

But I was not about to let him think he could bully me. "If you think you can put me back in my lane, you're welcome to get your scrawny ass over here and try."

I don't know what he saw in my eyes, but it was enough to make him look me up and down and realize I was a hell of a lot bigger than he. His social status wouldn't mean shit when I knocked out his teeth and put him in the hospital. Snapping his mouth shut, he wisely turned and went back into his house.

Disappointed, but content with the outcome of our little confrontation, I got behind the wheel and called Emily. She must have had her phone in hand, because it didn't even ring before she answered.

"Kaos? How did it go?"

"Made the drop. Chickenhawk signed."

Sounding relieved, she laughed. "Chickenhawk, huh?"

"Trust me, it's fitting. This shithead struts like a hawk, but clucks like a fuckin' chicken."

"An alive and uninjured chicken, I trust?"

"Yes ma'am. I was a model of self-restraint." I was so pissed I could barely get the words out. My hands shook as I started up the car. The fucker had gotten under my skin, and I needed to get out of there before I did something stupid like march my ass back into that house and put Matt Parker through a wall.

"You don't sound very restrained."

"I've played my hand and done my part. The game face is down. It took everything in me not to put my foot up his ass."

"We'll get him, Kaos. In a way that doesn't land you in jail and implicate Tina. I'll meet you at the fire station. You can let off some steam in the basement gym. I'll even call ahead, and Shari will have a strong drink waiting for you."

I turned the corner and stepped on the gas, getting as far away from temptation as possible as I headed for the Dead Presidents headquarters. "You're too good to me. See you soon, boss."

5

Tina

I KEPT ONE eye on the time as I used my phone's browser to check out the local help wanted ads. It was three-twenty-two p.m., which meant the first televised basketball game of the day had started. Where was Kaos? I pictured him turning into my neighborhood and getting an eyeful of the beautiful blue cage I'd broken free from.

God, I hated that house.

It was Matt's dream, but all I saw was a prison. And I'd stepped into that cell and locked myself in all too willingly. It hadn't started out like that. When I got pregnant with Dylan, I had every intention of finding a job as soon as he was born. But, without my degree, nothing paid enough to cover the cost of day care. Matt came from money and made more than enough to support us. I let him talk me into staying home until Dylan stopped breastfeeding. And then until he started kindergarten. Somewhere along the line, I stopped fighting for myself completely.

I couldn't argue with Matt's logic. Besides, when we'd lived in our old apartment building, being a stay-at-home mom hadn't been all bad. I'd made friends in the building, and my sister was within walking distance. Matt worked long hours, but I wasn't entirely by myself with Dylan when he was gone.

Then Matt surprised me with the house.

Most women would be over-the-moon at the immaculate modern kitchen and the giant walk-in closets, but all I saw was isolation. Duvall was twenty-five miles from my friends and sister, and I didn't have a car. Matt had grinned from ear to ear as he showed me around my pretty blue cage, but I felt the walls closing in on me.

Regardless, I didn't want to be miserable, so I tried to make the move work. I filled my lonely days with gardening, cooking, and interior design. Heck, I even tried to fit in with the catty, pretentious housewives of our upscale suburban neighborhood. But I hadn't come from money and couldn't care less who was carrying around a knock-off purse. No matter how I tried to keep busy, I missed my squad.

Even as my house and garden thrived, I withered away.

I begged Matt to sell the house and move us back into the city, but he never let my wants and needs get in the way of what he believed was best. Twisting my words and turning himself into a victim, he made me feel so damn ungrateful I hated myself for even making the suggestion.

After our fight that night, he left to get some air. Now, I couldn't help but wonder if he'd visited his prostitute. If she'd taken the beating he'd wanted to give to me. Had that been the first time? Or was it when he found out I'd gotten an IUD and didn't want to have any more children? Even back then I must have sensed something was... off with my husband.

Matt beat women. I'd seen the box of Polaroids with my own eyes, and had felt his fists against my skin, but I still had trouble wrapping my mind around his crimes.

I wasn't a perfect wife, but I'd tried. My efforts didn't matter. He'd been so desperate to beat the crap out of me that he'd found a whipping girl with my likeness. He said she was just a prostitute, but I wished I had a way to contact her so I could warn her. Who knew what he'd do to that poor woman once Kaos served him divorce papers?

He's gonna be so pissed. I should be packing.

Too bad I had nowhere to go. Even if I did, the old Mazda I'd paid cash for with my first post-Matt paycheck would be lucky to make it out of city limits, much less across state lines. The balance in my checking account could cover a couple of value meals and a tank of gas, but that was about it.

Maybe I should have waited to serve him papers until I was financially stable and ready to run, but that could take years, and I'd already given up so much of my life for Matt. I refused to give him one day more. I only hoped my haste to get free of him wouldn't come back to bite me in the butt.

"You okay over there?" my sister asked.

I'd been so deep in my thoughts I hadn't even heard Elenore come in. Still in her workout clothes, she went straight to the refrigerator and refilled her metal water bottle. Two years younger, four inches taller, and way more intelligent than I, my little sister had her life together. Since I'd moved away, she'd poured herself into her career and her health, and she was killin' it on the life front. I was happy for her, but her success could be a little intimidating at times. Especially when my life was in the toilet.

"Yeah, I'm fine," I lied. Fine was my go-to state of mind. If nobody was dead, it was fine. I could have a broken beer bottle sticking out of my gushing jugular, and still insist I was fine. It was a mindset, really.

"I'm fine, it's fine, everything's fine," She said, repeating my mantra in a sing-songy voice. "You, my sister, are plenty of things, but *fine* is not one of them."

Yeah, so I occasionally lied about my level of coping, and she called me out on it. That was kind of our thing.

"Are you calling me ugly?" I asked, trying my best to sound offended. Whenever lying didn't work on Elenore, I deflected.

"No. I'm calling your life a dumpster fire."

She had me there. I couldn't help but snort out a laugh as I shook my head. "Fair enough."

"Are you gonna keep trying to throw me off, or will you explain why you have a white-knuckled grip on that phone?" she asked. "By the way, that isn't the posture of someone who's fine. You look like you're waiting for a ransom caller to tell you where to drop off the money. Where's my nephew? He hasn't been kidnapped, has he?"

"No. He's moping in his room since I won't let him play video games."

"Uh oh." She guzzled down a long drink of water before wiping her mouth with the back of her hand. "Since it's the weekend, I know he didn't get in trouble at school again, so what'd he do this time?"

"He has so much attitude, and I can't handle it today."

She nodded. Dylan and Elenore had a great relationship that hadn't been affected by my impending divorce, but she'd seen how differently he treated everyone else. "How'd your appointment go yesterday?" she asked. She'd worked late yesterday, and by the time she got home, I was asleep. Then this morning she had errands to run before she hit the gym.

"Good. We got the papers filled out and came up with a plan to serve them to him."

Elenore paled and her gaze shot to my neck. "You scared of how he'll react?"

"I'm trying not to think about it while I look for a job."

"How's that going?"

I knew what she was really asking, but chose to focus on what I wanted to discuss. "Not great. I'm about as employable as a chimpanzee."

She grabbed an apple from the fruit basket and rinsed it. "You're in luck, then. Chimpanzees have been known to use tools and learn sign language, so there's hope for you yet." Not only did she let me have my distraction, she played along. I loved my sister so much.

"Gee, thanks. How do our primate friends fare against Microsoft Office and QuickBooks?"

"See, that's your problem. You're treating these programs like enemies rather than the helpful tools they are. Computers are friends, T."

"You don't know that. The machines could rise up at any time. I've seen the movies."

Elenore rolled her eyes and bit into her apple. My sister was a brilliant chemical engineer for a bigtime CBD manufacturer. To her, everything was a scientific equation she needed to solve, and I enjoyed driving her crazy by throwing out random conspiracy theories.

"Why are you looking for a new job?" she asked. "I thought Mr. Denali said you could return when your bruises are gone."

Mr. Denali was a financial advisor in his early sixties. Despite my anemic resume and creative writing attempt at a work history, he'd given me an entry-level job as a receptionist. The work was easy, the pay was better than nothing, and the hours worked around Dylan's school schedule. It had been the perfect fit until I'd gotten jumped in the parking garage.

The memory still made my blood run cold. Even worse, was the way the cops reacted to my attack. When they questioned Matt and discovered he had an alibi, they looked at me with suspicion, like I was some vindictive wife, trying to pin a random attack on my husband. Or maybe they thought I'd set the whole thing up. I had nothing to hide and had admitted I hadn't seen my attacker's face. It hadn't occurred to me that Matt's friends were as sleazy as he was and would lie to protect him.

"Come home, honey. You know you belong with me. Don't make me kill you."

I could still hear the words he'd whispered into my ear as he wrapped his fingers around my neck from behind. The scent of his cologne—something I'd once found soothing—flooded my senses and made tears of terror leak from my eyes. I didn't need to see his face to know who he was. The truth of his identity could be found in every squeeze of his hands.

"T?" Elenore nudged me.

I shook myself, trying to remember what we'd been talking about. My job. Right. "Yes, but I haven't been there long enough to accrue vacation or sick days, and you know I can't afford to miss work." I had trouble covering my bills as it was. If my check was any slimmer, I'd have to juggle my bills or make partial payments until I could catch up. If I ever could catch up.

"Yes, you can. I'll help you. Be honest with yourself, and with me. Why are you really looking for a new job?"

My sister always could see through my excuses and lies. "He knows where I work, El," I admitted, hating the fear in my voice. My hands had started to shake, so I lowered my phone to the table and hid them in my lap.

Elenore's eyes filled with compassion for a split second before anger lit it on fire. "I hate that manipulative bastard." Pushing away from the counter, she paced the kitchen. "You left him. He shouldn't be able to keep screwing with you like this."

"I know." I was so tired of dealing with Matt. The lies, the bruises, the false promises, the secrets… nine years of trying to keep my footing while his truths crashed against me had worn me down. My very being felt eroded, but the knot of anxiety in the pit of my stomach told me Matt wasn't done chipping away at me yet. Not by a long shot.

As if reading my mind, Elenore assured me, "You're safe here. He doesn't like witnesses, and he'd need someone to buzz him into the building."

"Right." I hope I sounded more convinced than I felt. She worked long hours, and usually Dylan and I were home alone. The building's security code access was more of a suggestion than anything. Tenants were known to prop open the door or kindly hold it open for the stranger behind them.

She swallowed and met my gaze. "I have some vacation time saved up. I can—"

"No. You are not using your vacation to babysit me."

"T—"

"No." I stood, folding my arms and meeting her gaze. "You've done more than enough. We'll be fine. I'll figure this out."

Elenore grabbed my hand, giving it a comforting squeeze. "Be careful. Every time you underestimate him, you get hurt."

I nodded. "I know. We shouldn't even be here. He knows where you live, and—"

"No." Now it was her turn to stare me down. "You have nowhere else to go. The bastard made sure of that. I've finally gotten you back, and he does not get to chase you away again. You're not putting me in danger, I'm choosing to help out my sister and nephew. I will always be in your corner, and nothing he says or does will change that."

My eyes burned as a sense of gratitude washed over me. Matt may have taken everything else from me over the years, but he couldn't touch my sister's devotion. "I love you," I said. "And I'm so lucky you're my sister."

"Damn straight." She grinned. "Besides, I've been killin' it in my kickboxing classes. I wish that asshole would make an appearance." Kicking the air in front of her, she spun around and threw a jab. "I'd like to show him what happens when he attacks a woman who's ready for him."

The sound of little footsteps interrupted her next spin kick. We turned to find Dylan wearing a sheepish expression as he slipped into the kitchen. His gaze met mine and he let out a dramatic sigh. "I've thought about my behavior, and I'm sorry."

Onto his act, I nodded. "Noted. Thank you. I forgive you, but you're still not playing video games tonight."

"Oh, come on!" He threw back his head and proclaimed his

frustration to the ceiling, humility façade gone. "I said I'm sorry. What more do you want from me?"

Elenore was trying not to laugh. I shot her a warning look before focusing on my son. "I'm glad you recognize what you've done and you're sorry, but there are still consequences for your actions. Your consequence is that you're not allowed to play video games today. Maybe you'll think about that before you act up next time."

"But I need to play NHL. I have to get really good at it, so I'll know what I'm doing when Kaos teaches me to play for real."

Elenore's eyebrows rose in question as she looked at me. "Chaos? Why on earth would we want Dylan learning chaos? Don't we have enough of that in our lives already?"

"Kaos is a big, tough biker who used to play hockey for the Sharks, Aunt El. He's gonna teach me how to play," Dylan said.

Something that could only be described as sheer panic flashed across Elenore's face. "A *biker*? You're going to let a big, tough biker teach Dylan how to play hockey?"

I'd been so stressed, wondering what Matt's reaction to the divorce papers would be, that I hadn't given much consideration to Kaos's offer. "I haven't decided if it's a good idea or not."

"Oh, it's a horrible idea," Elenore said, sounding scandalized.

At the same time, Dylan threw up his hands in exasperation and said, "Oh, give me a break."

My sister and I turned to stare at my little drama king.

"This is a good opportunity for me. If I work hard, I can make the NHL and buy you a house, Mom. A big one. And a car that doesn't suck. Aunt El, you can live with us, too," he said.

I pointed to him. "You. Back to your room. We'll discuss this later."

His shoulders dropped and he rolled his eyes, but he did turn and march back the way he'd come.

"He's not wrong," Elenore said. "Learning a sport from a pro is huge. But I think we should circle back to the whole biker thing. When did you start hanging out with bikers?"

My little sister's eyes were far too judgy for comfort, making me want to clap back. "Well, I started thinking that the best way to get rid of my ex is to find someone who's bigger and stronger to take him out, so I hit up a biker bar. Since I don't have any money, they were willing to let me trade my body for their services. I let them run a train on me, and—"

"Stop." Elenore's hand went up to silence me as her eyes about bugged out of her head. "You did what?"

I rolled my eyes. "God, El, I'm not a slut, and I'm not stupid. I've learned my lesson and plan to stay as far from men as possible. He's not a Hell's Angels type biker. He's a veteran. He was volunteering at Ladies First when I went in to sign the divorce decree. Dylan sat with him, and... I think they bonded somehow. He seemed nice. He told me he used to be a little brat, but hockey straightened him out. Thinks it'll do the same for Dylan. I have so much going on right now, I haven't had time to even consider the offer, but Dylan won't shut up about him."

"But why is his name Kaos?" Elenore enunciated each word. "That sounds like an earned name, making me wonder exactly how he acquired it. Is he destructive? Does he create disorder wherever he goes? More importantly, are you sure his offer was a suggestion? What if it was like one of those mobster situations... a deal you can't refuse. Will his buddies Mayhem and Anarchy show up on our doorstep to make sure we don't talk? Like ever again."

"Mayhem is a cool nickname!" Dylan said from the doorway.

Trying not to roll my eyes, I pointed. "Room. Now."

When I turned back to Elenore, she looked traumatized. No doubt she was imagining my little boy wearing leathers and chains and insisting people call him Mayhem. "You need to keep custody of Dylan," she warned. "If Matt finds out he's hanging out with some biker named Kaos, he's gonna have a cow."

"I know."

My phone rang.

I glanced at the screen and frowned. The caller was anonymous. Matt liked to call me from blocked numbers when he wanted to threaten or yell at me and didn't want a record of the call. He would have received the divorce papers by now and this had to be him, ready to rant and rave at me. I thought about sending the call to voicemail, but needed to know how he was handling the news and what I'd be dealing with.

"Speaking of the devil?" Elenore asked.

"Probably. Wish me luck."

"You don't need luck. You need a priest to exorcise that demon from your life."

Unfortunately, no priests were present. Clearing the fear from my throat, I answered the call, trying to keep my voice as steady as possible. "Hello?"

"All I ever wanted to do was love you," Matt said in my ear, his words clipped with anger. "Everything I've done has been for you and Dylan, and this is how you repay me? You give up? Our family means the world to me, and you're ripping it apart. Have you even thought about how this will affect Dylan? You grew up without a dad, and you know how hard that was on you. Do you really want to put him through that kind of pain?"

"No. If I did, I wouldn't have dropped out of college to be with you, Matt." I didn't want to fight him, but I couldn't sit through another one of his guilt trips, either.

"You hadn't even picked a major yet, and I have no idea how you planned to pay for school. I did you a favor. You owe me, Kristina."

"I gave you nine years of my life, and you wanted to hit me so bad, you found a hooker who looks like me to beat on. And then you turned your fists on me. I don't owe you anything."

He chuckled, and it sounded off. Forced. "You're just making shit up now. None of that happened, and you know it."

"I'm not the cops. You don't have to lie to me. I was there, remember? I suppose you're still claiming it wasn't you who jumped me after work?"

"I was at Chi-Chi's with Aaron and Dwight. Even the wait staff vouched for me," he said through gritted teeth. "I don't know what's going on in that twisted little brain of yours, but you need help. Maybe I should come get Dylan so you can get some rest and figure out why you're so damn desperate to destroy what I worked hard to build. You've always been a bit self-destructive, but this is getting ridiculous."

Matt never admitted guilt. Never. Instead, he always brought me over to his way of thinking, making me question my senses and feel like I was overreacting. But this time, he'd gone too far. I had a photograph of his abused hooker and had felt his anger first-hand. No matter what he said, I couldn't be persuaded to forget those horrors. His days of gaslighting me were over. "We both know your buddies would lie for you, and I'm sure you paid off a waitress to verify their story."

"You're the only one making shit up, and I'm worried about the safety of our son. He needs stability and quite frankly I don't think you can give it to him right now. Let me come and pick him up, and there will be no reason to involve the police. I can be at your sister's in thirty minutes."

The hair on the back of my neck stood up and every instinct screamed at me to grab Dylan and run. "You can't do that. You signed the agreement for supervised visits. You promised you wouldn't do this, Matt."

"That was before I realized how unstable you are. You're dangerous to Dylan, and without Elenore, you'd have no resources to provide for him. If this goes to court, you won't have the money to hire an attorney. You know I'll get him in the end. I always win. Might as well just hand him over now."

He didn't know I had other people in my corner now. Reaching into my pocket, I slid my fingers over the worn business card still there, reassuring myself. "I am not handing my son over to a woman beater," I spat.

"More lies." Matt clicked his tongue. "Such a disappointment. Maybe I should come over there and have a conversation with Elenore. Let her know what's really going on. Maybe she can help me get you the psychiatric help you obviously need."

My sister had never trusted Matt, and there was no way she'd believe him over me. Especially when she'd been the one to clean me up after his beatings. Still, I didn't miss the threat in his words. I'd never meant to put Elenore in danger, but now she was in his crosshairs. "I'm not staying with her anymore," I lied. "I moved out today."

The phone went quiet. As I started to wonder if he'd hung up, Matt chuckled, calling my bluff. "You don't have anyone else," he said confidently. "Nowhere else to go."

"Maybe you don't know everything there is to know about me," I replied.

"You better fuckin' be at Elenore's." Matt's voice had gone cold and low. He was done playing with me. "And when I come for you and Dylan, I expect you to comply. I don't care how delusional you are, your place is here. You are *mine*. You understand? *Mine!* Your little game is over, one way or another."

"You don't have the right to order me around anymore. I have to go. Don't bother looking, because you won't find me. Goodbye, Matt," I said, hitting the end call button. My hands trembled. Icy, invisible fingers slid up my spine as tears burned my eyes. My husband was going to kill me. I'd been stupid to think this could work… that I could get away from him. Now, he'd be coming for me. Coming to Elenore's.

I had to get out of there.

Elenore's arm slid around my waist, holding me up when I wanted to crumple to the floor and cry. "What did that bastard say?" she asked.

Before I could answer, my phone rang again. I was so startled, I almost dropped it. Emily's name popped up on the caller ID. I sucked down a breath, trying to get my heart to stop racing, and answered.

"Hey Tina. Great news. Kaos did it. Matt has officially been served. I'll get everything filed tomorrow morning. Congratulations, you are one step closer to getting your life back. In ninety days, you will officially be a free woman."

She sounded so cheerful and encouraging, but ninety days felt like an eternity to me. Especially when Matt was on his way to collect me and Dylan.

Going back to him wasn't an option.

"Tina?"

I tried to answer, but all I could do was sob.

"Ohmigod, what happened?" Emily asked. "Is he there? Are you safe?"

"I'm... he called. He knows where I am. He's coming. He's going to kill me."

Elenore's arm around my waist tensed, then squeezed, offering me her silent support. Resting her head on my shoulder, she covertly listened in on the conversation. Her presence was a comfort, and I let her be nosy and didn't pull away.

"No, he's not. We have resources. Just a sec." She spoke with someone in the background, but I couldn't make out their words. "My husband says there's room for you and Dylan at his club."

"His club?"

"His motorcycle club. It's in an old fire station and—"

"I can't take Dylan to a motorcycle club." I'd watched one episode of *Sons of Anarchy*, and that had been all the evidence I'd needed that kids didn't belong in those kinds of clubs. Agitated by the idea, by the whole situation, really, I stepped out of my sister's embrace and sat at the kitchen table.

"I can pick them up," a deep voice said in the background. It sounded like Kaos. "I have plenty of room at my house and my security system is top of the line. They'll be safe there."

"Kaos has a huge house," Emily said. "And he's offering to let you stay with him."

"I... I can't." I didn't even know Kaos. He seemed nice, but so had Matt, and look how that had turned out. My sister was watching me, her brow furrowed in worry as she tried to keep listening in. She was generous and amazing, and I didn't want to put her in danger by staying. I couldn't risk her.

"You can trust Kaos," Emily insisted. "He is a good guy, and he'll take care of you and Dylan. I know you're afraid, but I promised not to lie to you, Tina. That promise still stands. You are my client to protect and I wouldn't do anything to put you or your son at risk. Kaos has been vetted. I can send you his background check and his training certificates. He wants to help, and he's financially in a place where he can. Let him. Please let us help you. You have options. You are not alone. Please don't go back to that man. I don't think you will survive, and I don't want that on my conscience."

She sounded almost as desperate as I felt. It opened my eyes to the problem I'd created by going to her. Emily was in my corner. If I went back to Matt now, I'd not only be endangering myself, but I'd be spitting in the face of all she and Naomi had done for me. I finally had people who cared whether I survived, and I didn't want to disappoint them.

My head suddenly felt too heavy to hold upright. I rested my forehead on the table and replied, "Okay. I'll get us packed. How soon can he be here?"

6

Kaos

IT WAS A weekend and the fire station was active. When I arrived after serving the divorce papers to Matt, the common area was full of brothers, ol' ladies, and club girls. The pool tables and dart boards were packed, and Shari was pouring drinks behind the bar. She held one up for me, but I shook my head. The job wasn't done quite yet, but I had every intention of taking her up on that drink once it was. I slipped into Link's office and handed off the signed receipt to Emily.

"How'd he take it?" she asked, her expression worried. She had their toddler, Jameson, on her hip, and was bouncing to keep him moving and content as Link worked at his desk.

I told them about how Matt had tried to win me over to his side, insulted me, and then backed down.

"Son-of-a-bitch sounds nuttier than squirrel shit," Link said, closing his laptop and looking to his wife. "You sure she's safe with her sister?"

Emily frowned and plucked her cell phone from the top of his desk. She made a call, and as soon as she started talking, I knew something was wrong. Link could tell, too. He offered up the club as a haven, but Tina and Dylan needed someplace a little more stable.

"I can pick them up," I said without giving it a second thought. "I have plenty of room at my house and my security system is top of the line. They'll be safe there." My house made sense. It was the logical place to stash them. But more than that, I wanted them there. They'd had a rough shake of things, and I wanted the opportunity to make their lives a little easier.

Besides, Dylan would dig my house, and I kind of liked the idea of finally impressing that little punk.

Tina took some convincing, but while Emily talked, Link assembled a team. By the time the phone call ended, the office was full of brothers chomping at the bit and ready to do his bidding. This was my first time being included in a club op, and watching our president's Special Forces experience in action was pretty fucking impressive.

"Listen up," Link commanded. Everyone crammed into the space stopped what they were doing and focused on him. "The ladies have a case, and they need our help." He deferred to Emily.

She nodded her thanks and quickly filled us in on the phone call.

When she finished, Link cleared his throat and added, "So we need to get Tina and Dylan out of there before Matt shows up. This asshole has beat the shit out of his wife twice. It won't happen again. Not on our watch."

"Fuck no, it won't," Havoc added. The club's sergeant-at-arms was a big black man whom nobody fucked with. Projecting menace, he folded his arms across his chest and asked, "What do you need, Prez?"

"I need you to sit this one out. At least for now. We'll hit this job with stealth, speed, and tech." Link looked over the rest of the group. "Tap."

Tap stepped forward eagerly. "Yessir?"

"Go with Kaos to retrieve Tina and Dylan," Link replied. "Full stalker protocol."

Tap nodded and slid the backpack he'd been carrying over his shoulders. "Yessir. I'm ready."

I didn't know what stalker protocol entailed, but clearly, Tap did. He seemed prepared, and I was glad one of us knew what we were doing.

"I don't want to leave the sister vulnerable," Emily said as Jameson started to fuss. He got a handful of her long dark hair, and Link swept in, releasing the toddler's fist and taking him from his mom.

"We won't." Link settled Jameson against his shoulder, patting his back as he paced behind his desk. "Since Tina's told Matt she's no longer staying with her sister, we're gonna make that happen. We need to remove any and all traces of her and set up safety protocols that make the sister an unappealing target. Rabbit, you available to join the away team?"

"To swoop in and save a couple of women? Shit, boss, you don't even have to ask. Just call me Superman. You know I live for this," Rabbit said.

Link cracked a smile. "Yeah. Just don't go lookin' for your Lois Lane. We got a fuckin' job to do."

Rabbit threw his hands up, as if appalled that Link would even suggest such a thing.

Link picked up his phone and started mashing buttons. "I'm texting all three of you the address. Get there, get them out, make sure the sister's safe. I want Tina's car back here at the station. Tap, if you find a tracker on the car, keep it on there. It would make my day if that fucker shows up here looking for her."

"Yours and mine both," Havoc agreed, his expression dark and foreboding. The big guy didn't seem to care for being benched.

Tap nodded. "Ten-four."

"Morse, Hound, you're leading support. The club and all of our resources are at your disposal."

"Thank you, Prez," Morse said.

Emily typed something into her phone. "Morse, I just sent you a link to Tina's file. It contains everything we have on the ex."

"Got it," Morse replied, his fingers flying over his tablet. "I'll share the pertinent information with the Away Team, and the Home Team will come up with a plan to—"

"I don't want to know," Emily said, cutting him off. "Whatever it is, leave me out of it. And this time, don't put any new information in that folder."

Morse chuckled. "Knowledge is power."

"It's how you obtain your knowledge that the courts take exception to," Emily fired back. "You keep your knowledge, and I'll keep my plausible deniability."

Link met my gaze. "Thank you for volunteering your house, brother."

I nodded. "Not a problem. Whatever you need."

His expression hardened. "We'll iron out the details and let you know what's going on once Tina and Dylan are safely tucked away. Matt said he can get to her in thirty minutes, I want you there in ten. Go. Don't let that son-of-a-bitch reach her before we do."

He didn't need to tell us twice. Tap, Rabbit, and I ran for the door.

"Who's driving?" I asked as we hit the hallway. "All I have is my bike."

"We can take one of the loaners," Rabbit said.

He and Wasp ran the club's shop, Formation Auto Repair. The shop kept vehicles on hand for customers in need of a loaner while their car was being worked on. I'd spent some time with Rabbit, and he seemed like a bit of an odd duck with more energy than any grown man should have. It surprised me when Link chose him for this mission, but now, I got it. Rabbit had access to transportation, and if there was a problem getting Tina's car back to the club, he knew who was on duty and could call for a tow.

We could have easily run the few blocks to the shop, but since we were in a hurry, the three of us hopped on our bikes and burned rubber down the road. Before joining the club, I'd never been much of a motorcycle guy. Sure, I had a dirt bike I liked to do tricks on as a teenager, but I never would have picked two wheels over four. Navigating Seattle traffic and parking had converted me, and as we wove through the bunched-up cars waiting for the light, I was damn grateful for my Harley.

Rabbit skidded to a stop beside a little Jetta that had to be at least twice as old as Dylan, barely turning off his engine before racing to the building. Tap and I parked next to his bike, and when Rabbit emerged, he tossed a set of keys to me. "You're drivin,' Kaos. Tap will need to work, and I'm gonna take my bike. I can get there faster in case the motherfucker shows his face."

With loud, colorful tats covering both arms, and dressed in jeans and a dingy white T-shirt under his cut, Rabbit was a lot to take in. My size had intimidated Tina, but at least I didn't look like I was fresh out of the slammer and packing heat. To the best of my knowledge, Rabbit had never done any hard time, but he did usually have a 9mm holstered at his waist and kept a knife in his boot. If Tina found him standing on her doorstep, chances were she'd probably never open the door again.

"She spooks easily," I said.

Rabbit smiled. "Relax. This ain't my first rodeo, prospect."

But it *was* mine, and I was nervous enough for both of us. I gave him a nod.

"Morse already sent us his photo," Tap said, holding up his phone. "You see that piece of shit, I want one of his teeth as a trophy. Fuckin' wife beater." Shaking his head, he slid into the passenger's seat of the Jetta with his bag in his lap.

Rabbit looked far too excited about the prospect of beating someone senseless. Worried any altercations we started would affect Tina's case, I would have cautioned him against it, but as he'd pointed out, I was just a prospect. Questionable mental stability aside, Rabbit outranked me. Link trusted him, and I would, too.

Besides, I kind of wanted one of Matt Parker's teeth, myself. Of course, I would have preferred to be the one to remove it. Rabbit hopped on his bike and rocketed out of the parking lot. I slid behind the wheel of the old Jetta and tried my best to keep up, but he lost us before I made it to the end of the block.

Chuckling, Tap started up the navigation on his phone. Pointing in the direction Rabbit had gone, he said, "Speed," pointing at me, he added, "Stealth," and finger on his own chest, he said, "Tech."

"Ah." Now, I understood. Rabbit was to get there quickly, my job was to get the targets out safely and without a tail, and Tap would do what he did best. "Thanks."

Tap nodded, rummaging through his backpack. He pulled out a couple of gadgets and kept typing out stuff on his phone. I was tempted to ask what he was doing, but figured it was probably over my pay grade if not my head. If I needed to know, he'd clue me in. He pulled out a new cell phone, still in its box, and started fiddling with it.

In addition to Formation Auto Repair, the club owned the Copper Penny Bar and Grill, and had their hands in several businesses owned and run by club members and their ol' ladies, like Ladies First. Tap, Morse, and Hound worked a side hustle that had to do with internet security, but fuck if I knew anything about it. I was only privy to the limited information I needed to complete the tasks I was given. If I wanted to know more, I had to earn my member patch by proving my loyalty and commitment to the club.

The problem was, none of their businesses had any use for my unique skill set, which made proving myself damn near impossible.

When I first arrived, I decided to try my hand at driving one of Formation's tow trucks. Havoc took me a safe distance out of town and let me get behind the wheel. I'd never driven anything bigger than my Escalade, and I struggled with the additional controls and wide turning radius, almost landing us in a ditch. The thought of navigating that beast through Seattle's narrow streets and insane traffic had me sweating buckets and made my ass cheeks clench so hard I thought I'd turn into one giant hemorrhoid.

Turned out a tow truck driver, I was not.

Determined to find something I didn't suck ass at, Link moved me to the Copper Penny. Flint, the bar manager, didn't really need me, but he had a couple of the guys train me to work security anyway. Now, I filled in on occasion, but keeping the peace by bouncing drunks out on their asses had gotten me no closer to earning my patch. Before Naomi asked me to help out at Ladies First, I was feeling pretty fucking useless to the club and wondering how the hell I'd ever prove my loyalty.

Over the past two days, I'd done more for the club than I had in the entire six months I'd been a prospect. It was nice to feel like I was part of something important again.

"You guys do this often?" I asked, watching Tap out of the corner of my eye as I drove.

He gave me a wry smile. "Do what?"

"Help Ladies First hide a woman."

He shrugged. "Some. Usually their clients don't have kids, so we stash the women at the fire station. Any dumbfuck stupid enough to try the club would be in for one hell of a surprise. You saw what it was like in that office. We have no love for women beaters. Emily keeps us on a tight leash for legal reasons. She has good instincts. She only calls us in when shit's about to go sideways. We're always prepared and uh... enthusiastic."

Most of my club brothers seemed like hotheads to me, but Tap painted them in a different light, making them seem experienced, competent, and able to follow orders. I hoped he was right. "Good to know. What's the plan? Anything special I need to do?" I asked.

Tap shook his head, but his gaze didn't leave the screen as he continued to work. "Focus on getting Tina and Dylan out of the condo and to your house. We'll do the rest."

I wanted details, but Tap was busy, and I didn't think he'd appreciate me distracting him with questions. Keeping my speed somewhere just south of reckless endangerment, I made good time. Tap gestured me into an underground parking garage, using his cell phone to snap pictures of the security cameras and other seemingly random things. It struck me once again how big time some of the Dead Presidents were. Sure, I'd been a professional hockey player, but there were rumors that this man used to work for the CIA. Link and Havoc were former Special Forces, and Morse... Morse had been a drone pilot and I didn't even know what else. He sure as hell hadn't picked up his insane hacking skills from flying remote-controlled aircraft for the Air Force.

Besides being smart and skilled, they were genuinely good people. Not a one of them had met Tina or Dylan, but they were all committed to keeping them safe. Not only because it would make Emily happy, but because it was the right thing to do. They were the kind of men who'd joined the military to help people. My story wasn't quite so noble. I didn't deserve to be among their ranks, but was determined to carve myself out a spot.

Regardless, my desire to get patched in had nothing to do with why I'd offered up my house as a refuge. No, my motivation was far more selfish than that. Tina's intense hazel eyes and lush curves had been tugging at my thoughts since the moment I laid eyes on her, and I wanted to figure out why.

Also, something primal inside me needed to know she was safe.

She was a single mom trying to get away from the piece of shit she was still married to. A smarter man would steer clear of that kind of drama, but for some reason, I couldn't. The woman hadn't given me the slightest hint she was interested in me, but it didn't matter. Every time I closed my eyes, I saw her intense hazel eyes staring back at me.

Maybe the altruistic spirit of the Dead Presidents was rubbing off on me, but I didn't think so. I only hoped we weren't too late to help her.

7

Kaos

AS WE NAVIGATED the underground parking garage, Tap pointed to a tan Mazda that looked like it had seen more turns around the sun than I had. "There. That's Tina's car. Park in the nearest visitor spot."

I did as I was told, and we both got out. Shouldering his backpack of goodies, he followed me. We found Rabbit leaning against the front of the building not far from the entryway. He peeled off the wall and joined us, flicking away the toothpick he'd been chewing on.

"No sign of the motherfucker," he said, sounding disappointed.

I called up to the unit. A woman answered. It didn't sound like Tina, but I wasn't sure.

"Hi. It's Kaos. I'm here for Tina and Dylan."

"Fine," she snapped, her tone unnecessarily hostile. "Come on up."

The security door unlocked with a loud buzz. I opened the door and headed in with the guys behind me. Tap kept snapping pictures of God-only-knew-what as Rabbit watched me with open curiosity.

"Hmm," he said as we headed toward the elevators. "'Magine that."

"Imagine what?" I asked, bracing myself for whatever shit he was about to flick me.

"You being a hotshot hockey player and all, I thought you'd be better with the ladies, but it sounds like they hate you almost as much as they hate me." Rabbit grinned as he entered the elevator and paused at the number pad. "Fourth floor, right?"

Tap nodded, and Rabbit pushed the button. The doors closed.

"I think that was Tina's sister," I replied, unsure why I felt the need to defend myself. "I haven't met her."

Rabbit cocked his head to the side and smirked at me. "You got any sisters, Kaos?"

I shook my head. "Nope. Just brothers."

"Well, I do, and if some motherfucker named Kaos showed up to take my sister to safety, he'd have to fight me, first. You should have given her your real name or something. Made yourself sound more respectable and a little less... chaotic and shit."

Tap arched an eyebrow at Rabbit. "Her husband's name is Matt. Sounds innocuous as fuck, but he still beat the shit out of her."

The elevator doors opened, and we exited.

"Yeah, I get that," Rabbit said. "But I still wouldn't hand my sister over to someone named Kaos."

Ignoring Rabbit, I found the unit number and knocked.

The door opened far enough to reveal an engaged chain and a sliver of the woman on the other side of the door. The chain might have made her feel safe, but it looked flimsy as hell. Any one of us could have dropped a shoulder and plowed right through it without much more than a bruise to show for our trouble.

"There's no way that'll stop Matt," I said to Tap.

He nodded, snapping a picture.

From what little I could see of her, the woman on the other side of the door wasn't happy to see us. Narrowing her visible eye at me, she said, "You must be Kaos."

Someone had described me. Wondering if it was Tina or Dylan, I nodded. "Yes ma'am. It's a pleasure to meet you... uh..."

I waited for her to provide her name, but she didn't. Instead, her gaze swiveled to take in my companions. "Why did you bring these two?"

Tap stepped forward, swinging his backpack down his arm. "Because we don't know what Matt Parker is capable of and we always come prepared. We're professionals. You must be Elenore. Your sister is lucky to have you looking out for her, but she's not safe here. I've already made out three ways I could have breached this building, and if we didn't respect you and the law, we'd be through that door before you could shout a warning. That little chain sure as shit wouldn't stop us. To my understanding, Matt has no respect for you or the law. He's unstable, and if he wants to get to Tina here, he will. From what I've seen, you won't be able to stop him."

Elenore stiffened. Tap's warning struck home so hard she didn't even try to deny it.

He unzipped his pack and propped it against the door, opening it wide enough so she could see inside. "We plan to take Tina to a more secure location but have no intention of leaving you alone and vulnerable. My name is Tap, and I have security equipment I'd like to discuss with you. Our club is called the Dead Presidents. We're veterans who have made vows to serve, protect, and aid the people of our community. Time is of the essence, but if it makes you feel more comfortable, you should google us and find out what we're about."

"I've heard of the club." Her expression turned thoughtful. "My company contributed to your toy drive last year." She turned her gaze toward Rabbit. "What about you? Why are you here?"

"The name's Rabbit." He gave her a wide smile. "My little sister once dated a guy who smacked her around. I was in Afghanistan at the time and couldn't do shit about it. By the time I got home, the motherfucker was in jail for armed robbery. I can't get to him in the slammer, but I have a lot of feelings about what he did to Rose. I'd like to take those feelings up with someone, and if this Matt Parker clown shows up, he'd make a good target. I'll protect you and your sister the way I wish someone would have protected mine."

Shocked, Tap and I both stared at Rabbit. I hadn't known about his sister and it was clear Tap hadn't either. Maybe there was more to the energetic, mouthy, slightly crazed mechanic than I'd previously assumed.

"I'm sorry to hear about your sister," I said.

Rabbit waved me off. "It was a long time ago. Now I have brothers to watch my back and protect my family when I can't."

The door closed. Metal scraped against metal, and then it swung open and Elenore stood in the doorway. Like her sister, she was a brown-haired, hazel-eyed beauty. Wearing sneakers, leggings, and a tank top, her hair up in a ponytail, she was built like a ballet dancer, tall and lithe. Rabbit's gaze raked over her body and his jaw dropped.

She eyed him skeptically before facing me. "Tina and Dylan are almost done packing and will be out in a minute. Dylan doesn't know what an abusive piece of shit his dad is, so please watch what you say in front of him."

Now it was my turn to gape as I wondered how she could possibly believe that bullshit. Dylan was smart and observant. Matt had left bruises on Tina twice. Regardless of whatever lies Dylan had been told to cover up the truth, that kid knew damn well where his mom got those bruises. I'd bet my left nut on it. Still, I wasn't there to make waves or point out the obvious, so I snapped my mouth shut and agreed. "Yes ma'am."

Tap spun around and snapped a few pictures of the door locks before joining us in the living room. "Where do you want me to set up?" he asked Elenore.

"Kitchen." She gestured toward a doorway before eyeing me and Rabbit. "You two can have a seat in here and wait."

Although her grey leather sectional looked cozy, I wasn't a have-a-seat-and-wait type of guy. Besides, I had different orders and was anxious to follow them. "You sure they won't need help with their luggage?" I asked.

Elenore frowned. "Maybe. One sec." She hurried down the hall and disappeared from sight.

"Nice place," Rabbit said. Settling on the chaise portion of the sectional, he kicked up his feet to get comfortable. I shook my head, hoping the grease from his jeans didn't stain the leather. Someone had left an open magazine on the seat cushion. He picked it up and angled the page toward me. "Water Soluble CBD Creates a Clear Solution," he said, reading the article title out loud. "Think she reads this shit for fun?"

Tap had already disappeared through the kitchen doorway, leaving me alone to deal with Rabbit. I shrugged, because I didn't care what Elenore was into. I was itching to get out of the condo before Matt showed up, saw me, and all hell broke loose. As much as I'd like to flatten the bastard, I didn't want to think about how that would affect Dylan.

Elenore appeared in the hallway with a suitcase in hand and a bag slung over her shoulder. I hurried over to lighten her load. As I took the bags, Tina emerged. I'd been expecting tears and hysterics about having to leave the comfort of her sister's condo, but when her gaze met mine, resolve and determination stared back at me. She was okay. I didn't realize how worried I'd been, but the wave of relief that washed over me confirmed that my emotions had gotten all wrapped up in this woman's plight.

"It's good to see you again," I blurted out. There should be nothing good about it. I was only there because Matt had threatened her safety, which made my statement sound really fucking thoughtless. "Not under the circumstances, of course, but I'm glad you're okay."

She dropped her gaze. "Thank you for coming for us."

"I told you, we help people. Whatever you need."

Dylan emerged with a backpack over his shoulder, rolling a suitcase behind him. His gaze landed on me and a grin lit up his face before he caught himself and schooled his expression. Giving me a very cool, very masculine lift of his chin, he greeted me with a simple, "S'up Kaos?"

The kid could try to hide it as much as he wanted, but he was happy to see me. He appeared almost relieved. Fighting back my own smile, I returned his chin lift. "S'up Dylan?" Turning my attention back to Tina, I said, "Let's get you guys out of here."

Tina frowned at Rabbit, who was watching our exchange from the comfort of the sectional. He set the magazine down and stood, offering her a smile.

"This is Rabbit," I said, ushering her and Dylan forward. "Tap's in the kitchen. They're going to help your sister out with security and make sure she's safe."

Tina tensed. "You want me to leave my sister alone with two strange men?"

When she put it like that, her hesitancy made sense. "Rabbit's the only strange one. Tap's perfectly normal," I said, trying to add a little levity to the situation.

Rabbit took a mock swing at me, but I easily pivoted out of his range.

"I'll be fine," Elenore said, giving her sister a wave with something that looked like a Taser in her hand. I was certain she hadn't been carrying that thing when she let us in, which meant Tap had equipped her as soon as she'd walked into the kitchen.

Tap came up behind Elenore and introduced himself to Tina and Dylan. "Tina, before you leave, I need to fill you in on what to expect. Would it be all right if Kaos and Dylan take the bags to the car while we chat?"

Dylan slid closer to his mom, glaring daggers at Tap and Rabbit. Regardless of how happy he'd been to see me, he wasn't about to leave his mom and aunt alone with strangers. Despite the fact I had no claims on the kid, a bizarre sort of pride swelled in my chest. He had a lot more going for him than people realized.

Tina turned toward me and raised her eyebrows, silently deferring to me.

"Tap and Rabbit are good, and they know what they're doing," I said. "You can trust them."

"I'll help load up the car," Rabbit offered, grabbing a couple of bags. To Dylan, he added, "I know Tap looks tough, but he's a fu... a frickin' nerd. He's about to talk their ears off about locks, video cameras, and alarm systems. I've heard it all before and it's boring as hell. Trust me, man, you don't want to have to sit through his spiel. Besides, if he gets out of line, your aunt can tag him with the Taser he just loaned her. I think I'd like to see that."

Tap frowned at Rabbit.

Dylan didn't look convinced, but Tina pushed him toward us. "We'll be fine. Help the guys."

Dylan stopped long enough to point a finger at Tap. "You better be nice to Mom and Aunt El."

Tap held his hands up in the universal sign of surrender. "You have my word. Man to man."

That seemed to appease Dylan. He followed Rabbit to the door as I grabbed the rest of the luggage and joined them, stopping to give Tina one last reassuring smile before I slipped out.

8

Tina

TAP WAS A handsome, muscular man with caramel-colored skin and a kind smile. The guys hadn't been there long, but he'd already equipped my sister with a Taser, leveling the playing field so she wouldn't feel quite so helpless with strangers invading her home. It was a brilliant move, really, and I could tell Elenore was warming up to him already.

"You should see the stuff he has in his backpack," she whispered to me as we followed Tap into the kitchen. "These guys are legit."

Her endorsement put me at ease, and I sat across the table from Tap. Elenore played host and got us all water.

"Thank you for trusting us. I know this can't be easy for you," Tap said.

"I don't have much of a choice," I replied. God, I sounded like an ungrateful hag. Shaking my head, I tried again. "I'm sorry. That came out wrong. The way you've all jumped through hoops to help us is... I can't thank you enough. I'm just angry and frustrated that Matt put us in this position."

"He'll get his." Tap rifled through his backpack. "They always do in the end. Especially when we intervene. Look, I'm not good at small talk, and quite frankly, we don't have time for it, so I'm going to jump right into the thick of things. Your cell phone is the easiest way for Matt to track you. I'm sure you don't want to give it up, and we won't make you, but it's the smart thing to do." He pulled a boxed iPhone out of his bag and set it on the table. "I won't leave you without a phone. I've added contact information for me, Kaos, and our club leader, Link, into this one. It's prepaid for the month with unlimited data. I can have your contacts transferred over. We just ask that you only share the number with the people who absolutely have to have it."

I nodded, eyeing the phone. It was a much newer model than my refurbished one. "That's very generous of you." Still, my phone was the way I stayed connected. Since leaving Matt, I'd been rebuilding friendships with the women I'd previously neglected, and the idea of disappearing on them again made my stomach sink. Pulling my phone out of my jacket pocket, I hesitated. In addition to the contact information for my friends, it held priceless pictures of Dylan and Elenore. "Will I get this phone back?"

"Yes. And I'll backup all your photos and texts in a secure location just in case something happens to it."

"Thank you." It was just a phone. A possession. I wasn't emotionally attached to it. I handed him mine, and then squeezed the boxed phone into my purse.

He nodded, tucking my phone away into a pocket of his backpack. "I'll keep this one charged and active at the club headquarters. Trust me, if Matt tracks it there, he'll regret it."

"I have a request," Elenore said, joining us at the table. "Any altercations your club has with that asshole... I want them recorded. Seriously. Watching a bunch of bikers beating the crap out of him is all I want for my birthday next month."

"We'll see what we can do," Tap said with a smirk. "Tina, I'd like to take your car to the station as well."

"My car?" My hard-earned independence felt like it was slipping away. I'd done this before—giving up my freedom because some man wanted to take care of me—and that had blown up in my face. I didn't know if I had it in me to trust like that again.

"She just got a car. You can't take it from her," Elenore said as if reading my mind. She grabbed my hand. "That's the kind of shit *he* did to her."

Tap's eyes softened. "I understand, and I won't be taking anything away. I only want to park it at the fire station until we get this situation under control. Tina, you are still technically married, and Washington is a community property state. I'm sure Matt knows about the car. He can report you missing and have the police search for it. If they find it at the club, we can handle the fallout, but we don't want anything to lead Matt to you and Dylan. Kaos has a very nice Escalade that I'm sure he'll let you borrow whenever you want. Hell, he let Spade use it last week to chauffeur his little sister and her date to prom. If he's using it, the club can loan you a car. This isn't about taking away your freedom. You won't be locked in the house or any of that bullshit."

"I want to know where she'll be staying," Elenore announced.

"Are you sure that's wise?" Tap fired back. "No offense, but I doubt you've been trained to watch for a tail. We have. Any time you want to see your sister, we can bring her to you and keep you both safe. Then we can make sure nobody follows her back to Kaos's."

Elenore frowned. "Good point."

"Tina, I also want to check your purse for tracking devices, if that's all right." He removed some sort of electronic contraption from his bag.

Elenore squeezed my hand. "You don't have to do this, T. You and Dylan can stay here, and we can call the cops if Matt shows up."

My sister meant well, but she didn't know how shady Matt

could be. "Until he jumps me in our parking garage and finishes what he started outside of work?" I said flatly.

Elenore's expression fell. "I wish I would have been with you that day."

I didn't. Who knew what other tricks Matt had up his sleeve? I couldn't live with myself if he hurt my sister to get to me. "You've done enough, El. You're amazing, and I don't know what I would have done without you for the past seven months. Tap here seems like he knows what he's doing, and I trust Kaos." Which was odd considering I'd never felt safe with Matt. Living with him had been like walking on eggshells. One wrong step, and he'd grow quiet and withdrawn, milking the codependent guilt he elicited. Or he'd become passive aggressive, his nasty barbs and tones making me feel like a horrible wife. I'd spent so much time tying myself in knots to keep him happy and maintain the peace. And for what? So I could end up here, relying on the kindness of strangers to keep me safe?

"T?" Elenore asked, squeezing my hand again to draw me from my thoughts.

Frustration made me want to scream. This was the bed I'd made. I'd laid in it when I decided to stay with him and make things work for Dylan's sake. Now, the bed was burning, and the firemen had arrived. I could either trust them to get me out of danger, or watch my world turn to ash.

And most likely take Elenore and Dylan down with me.

Handing my car keys off to Tap, I slid the strap of my purse down my arm and set it on the table, opening it wide. "Do your worst."

Tap took a deep breath and his shoulders relaxed. Relief flooded his eyes, and he gave me a wide, genuine smile. Like Kaos, this man obviously cared what happened to me and my son, and was being considerate and careful of not only my physical safety but also my emotional comfort. The realization stung my eyes and formed a lump in my throat. They might look a little scary, being

Centering Kaos

big, tatted bikers and all, but these were the good guys, and I'd somehow been lucky enough to find them.

After thoroughly scanning my purse and pocketing my keys, Tap gave Elenore a reassuring smile. "I promise you we will protect them. And you. Now, let's talk about your security."

Tap and Elenore were deep in negotiations about alarm systems and cameras when the guys returned. My sister stood and hugged me and Dylan goodbye as Rabbit sat in my abandoned seat at the table. I didn't miss the way he checked Elenore out as she returned her attention to Tap. My strait-laced sister had an inked-up biker admirer. Now that was interesting.

"You ready to go?" Kaos asked, leaning against the doorframe.

I nodded, not trusting myself to speak.

Dylan surprised me by sliding his hand into mine and tugging me past Kaos and toward the door. "It's gonna be okay, Mom."

Tears flooded my eyes. Hoping he was right, I blinked them back and let myself be led into our new reality.

Kaos lived in Northeast Seattle, at the end of a private road, positioned on a hill and surrounded by evergreens. It was almost fully dark by the time we arrived, but bright interior lights illuminated giant windows. The modern, boxy, black and grey exterior was elegant and unique. Stunning. I'd never seen anything like it.

"Whoa, you live here?" Dylan asked, his face pressed against the window and his eyes wide as we idled on the stone driveway.

"Yep." Kaos tugged a set of keys out of his pocket, and the garage door opened, revealing enough space for two cars beside a shiny black Escalade.

I had started out the drive feeling like a nervous wreck, but Kaos had kept me and Dylan talking, slowly draining the tension from our situation with his easy-going nature and incredible sense of humor. We hadn't really chatted about anything important—just the city, its attractions, and our favorite foods—but the conversation was nice. Relaxing. Despite his massive size, striking good looks, and history as an NHL player, he was a modest, easy-to-talk-to, down-to-earth guy.

"It looks like someone stacked a bunch of giant boxes on top of each other and added windows," Dylan said, still eyeballing the house as we rolled into the garage and parked. "But in a good way. This is a cool house."

Kaos turned toward me, his eyes wide with mock wonder and his smile infectious. "Did I really just get a compliment from the ruthlessly blunt Dylan Parker?"

Having worked my butt off for one of those elusive compliments myself, I fully understood Kaos's sarcastic wonder. Unable to help myself, I laughed. "It is a beautiful home, but his compliments are a little terrifying, am I right?"

"Feels like winning the lottery but knowing it's gonna change your tax bracket and you'll have to pay back more than you won."

He was so funny, direct, and dead-on correct. "Yes. That's it exactly."

"Are you guys talking about me?" Dylan asked.

I shook my head no, but Kaos answered truthfully, "Of course. Who else would we be talking about?"

Dylan seemed too distracted to care. He hurried out of the car, stopping to gape at the Escalade we'd parked beside. "Nice ride! Why do you even have this ugly old car? You should have picked us up in that one."

"Dylan!" I snapped, embarrassed by his rudeness.

Kaos chuckled. "Annnd he's back." He closed his door and patted the roof of the ugly old car in question. "This is a loaner from the club. My Escalade was here, and I couldn't very well fit you and your mom on the back of my Harley."

Dylan's eyes widened as he spun around in circles, searching. "You have a Harley? Where is it?"

"At the club. I'll pick it up tomorrow when I drop off the Jetta."

"Will you take me for a ride?"

My heart leapt out of my chest as images of motorcycle crashes flashed through my mind, "No," I said firmly.

"Come on, Mom," Dylan whined.

Kaos popped the Jetta's trunk. "Don't give your mom a hard time. She makes the rules. Help me take the luggage in so I can show you your room."

Surprisingly enough, Dylan let the matter drop and joined Kaos. I flashed the man a grateful smile, and he nodded back. I rounded the car to help them with the luggage, but Kaos waved me off, insisting they had it under control. I followed him inside with Dylan behind me.

Kaos stopped to disengage the security system, and I stepped into the entryway to get my first glimpse of our temporary home. Pristine white walls and gorgeous pale wooden floors drew my attention. I could feel Kaos's gaze on me as I took in the high ceilings and open floor plan of the living room. Kaos dropped his keys in a bowl on the ebony entry table and gestured me around the corner. Floor to ceiling windows covered most of the walls, and I could see nothing but darkness outside.

I tensed, suddenly worried about what could be out there looking at me. "Whoa. Don't you feel exposed?" There wasn't a single curtain in sight.

Kaos shook his head. "Nope. All that's out there is my backyard, and then a cliff. The yard's fenced and surrounded by evergreens, so nobody can see in."

The only portion of the wall not broken up by windows held a metal sheet that stretched from the floor to the ceiling with a gas fireplace insert.

"That's unique." I slid closer to get a better look. "And gorgeous." I spun around. "This whole room is incredible."

"Thanks," Kaos said, sounding strangely nervous. "I wanted something... different, and the moment I saw this place, I knew it was perfect. Plenty of space, lots of daylight, low maintenance yard. I'll have to show you that tomorrow when it's light outside."

Overstuffed light grey sofas covered in throw pillows were situated around the fireplace, and before I realized what he was doing, Dylan dropped his luggage and jumped on the nearest sofa. Pillows flew everywhere as he bounced.

Horrified by his behavior, I yelled at him to stop. He turned to give me his best innocent face. "What? I wanted to see how comfortable it is."

"We don't jump on furniture," I admonished. "Apologize to Kaos."

"Sorry, Kaos." Dylan dropped his gaze with a pout.

"He doesn't get out much," I said by way of explanation. Truthfully, neither of us did, and we'd never been anywhere as nice as this house. The pale floors were unnerving, and I couldn't stop imagining Dylan's muddy footprints all over them.

Kaos patted my back. "Don't worry. All the furniture's made of damn sturdy material. Has to be, or my nieces and nephews would have destroyed it all months ago."

I tried really hard to listen to his words, but all my attention had homed in on the hand on my back. Warmth poured from the contact, sending all kinds of signals I wasn't prepared for throughout my body. When was the last time a man had touched me? Matt and I hadn't had sex in close to eight months, but there was no intimacy with him. He'd surely never made my stomach flutter like this.

"I want you to make yourselves comfortable here." Kaos's hand dropped possessively to my lower back as he turned me away from the fireplace. "Come on. I'll show you the rest of the main floor."

When we reached the kitchen, he dropped his hand, and I felt both relieved and disappointed by the loss of his touch. Trying not to overanalyze my reaction, I took in the dark wood cabinets, pale quartz countertops, and matching stainless-steel appliances. A massive fridge was tucked away near the side-by-side gas range, both of which were surrounded by more counter space than I'd ever seen in a kitchen. Five upholstered stools were tucked under the breakfast bar, and the dark wood table in the adjoining dining room sat twelve.

"You live alone?" I asked, unable to keep the disbelief out of my voice.

Kaos nodded. "I have a big family and we get together often. Sometimes I host."

"Do you cook?"

"For myself. Occasionally. I mean, I try." He looked away. "Okay, none of that is true. I'm on a first name basis with all the local Uber Eats, DoorDash, Grubhub, and restaurant delivery people. According to my mother, I am a menace in the kitchen."

"But this kitchen! How can you own a kitchen like this and not want to cook?"

"Don't get me wrong, it's not the desire I lack, it's the skill. I love my house. I don't want to burn it down."

After living with a man who believed himself to be perfect, there was something so endearing about Kaos's self-deprecating humor, I couldn't help but lean closer to him. "I'm sure it's not that bad."

"Are you underestimating my ability to cause mass destruction?"

Was he flirting with me? It had been so long, I couldn't tell. It felt good, though, and a smile tugged at my lips. "I would never. I mean your name is Kaos, after all."

"Technically, my name is Darius."

Pleased that he'd given me his real name, I held out a hand. "Nice to meet you, Darius."

Both grinning, we shook.

"Did Kaos come from the military?" I asked.

"No." He leaned against the bar. "My first coach gave me that. I told you I had some problems with my temper growing up. Whenever Coach heard I was acting out off the ice, he would bench me. I wanted to play, so I got really good at suppressing my anger. Then, as soon as the puck was in play, I'd let it all out. It felt like a balloon being popped. The pressure propelled me all over the place. Coach said it was like I was everywhere all at once, checkin,' passin,' scorin,' causin' chaos everywhere I went. One day, he started calling me Kaos and it stuck."

My gaze drifted to Dylan who was pressed up against one of the floor-to-ceiling windows with his hands cupped around his face, trying to see outside. "Mom, you have to see the yard," he shouted. "It looks so cool!"

"You think it'll be like that for Dylan?" I asked.

Kaos shrugged. "Every kid's different. But I can promise you that learning how to play with a team won't hurt him. Now that you're here, I can take him out on the ice and see what he thinks. A buddy of mine coaches at one of the local arenas. He'll have some gear we can borrow."

Before I could answer, Dylan came shooting into the room, skidding to a stop in front of me. "Mom! Kaos has a game room!"

I hadn't even seen him leave the window. "A game room?"

The heat of Kaos's hand returned to my lower back. "Yeah. Come on, I'll show you."

As we walked, he pointed out a bathroom and an office before rounding the corner and stepping down into a sunken great room. It was the size of his kitchen and living room combined, with more overstuffed sofas angled toward a large screen television, a dart board, pool table, foosball table, an air hockey table, and a bookshelf loaded with board games.

"This is the coolest room ever!" Dylan announced, bouncing as he hustled past me to check out the tables.

"Another compliment?" Kaos asked, sounding amused.

I bit back a smile. "Don't get used to it. The newness will wear off soon. Let me guess, this room is for your nieces and nephews, too?"

"Nope." Kaos stepped up to the foosball table and spun one of the rods attached to the little soccer players. "This is all for me, but I let them play with me occasionally."

The sound of the spinning rod caught Dylan's attention, and he leaped halfway across the room to join Kaos. "Can I play?"

"Ask your mom," Kaos said, deferring to me.

"One game, and then we need to find you a bathtub and a bed."

"But I took a bath yesterday," Dylan complained.

"Kaos is being nice and letting us stay at his house, so we need to take care of it. You don't want to leave the bed stinking like your sweaty feet, do you?" I asked. Dylan had the worst smelling feet on the planet if he didn't bathe daily. I was hoping that was something he'd grow out of eventually.

"Gross," Kaos added.

Dylan sighed. "Fine. I'll bathe."

Kaos's lips twitched, but he managed not to smile as he dropped a little white ball in the middle of the foosball table. The two of them started spinning rods and calling out challenges, and by the end of the game, Dylan was belly laughing. I couldn't remember the last time I'd seen tears of joy leak from his eyes and my chest squeezed at the sight.

"Did you see that?" he asked me, pointing to the table. "Kaos accidentally kicked the ball into his own goal."

I was pretty sure the last goal hadn't been accidental, but there was no way I'd wipe the smiles off of either of their faces by saying as much. "Yeah. That was crazy. Come on now. Let's go find you a bathtub."

Dylan looked to Kaos for help.

Kaos stepped forward and mussed his hair. "We'll have plenty of time to play tomorrow."

"After school," I amended.

Kaos smiled. "After school."

The guys grabbed the bags and we headed upstairs. Dozens of framed photographs covered the wall of the stairwell. Dirty-faced kids throwing up peace signs and sneaking bunny ears behind each other. A giant group gathered in front of Disneyland. Smaller group family photos. Elderly looking grandparent types seated in front of a Christmas tree and surrounded by what had to be generations of kids and grandkids.

"Wow," I said, taking it all in. "You said your family was big, but... This is all family, right? You didn't just buy a bunch of frames and keep the stock photos that came with them, did you?"

Kaos chuckled. "Nope. I wish some of them were stock photos, but no. These are all related to me through blood or marriage. Bunch of crazies. To be honest, I joke, but I wouldn't trade them for the world." His smile was proud as he pointed to a dark-haired couple. "These are my parents. I'm sure you'll meet my mom soon. She likes to pop in from time to time and make sure my fridge is stocked. My cousin shops and cleans for me—and Mom knows this—but I've learned life is a lot easier if I let my mom do what she wants."

I elbowed Dylan, hoping he was paying attention. "You hear that? That's wisdom right there."

"Are your parents local?" Kaos asked, watching me.

I didn't want to talk about such a sad subject. With a family this enormous, he probably had a hard time understanding that some people had no one. It probably seemed strange to him that my family hadn't stepped in to deal with Matt, or to help me out. I wanted him to understand why. "No. My dad's... he left shortly after Elenore was born and didn't look back. Mom died in a car accident when I was fifteen. It's been me and Elenore ever since. Well, until I got pregnant."

Kaos frowned. "Did you go into the foster system?"

"No. Mom's brother, Uncle Ralph, took us in. He wasn't much of a kid person, but he and his wife made sure we were fed and educated. They moved to Arizona after Elenore graduated. Did their duty and split. We're not really close." I didn't mean to air my family's dirty laundry, but I was afraid he'd think I was a bad person

Centering Kaos

who'd burned my bridges. My bridges were intact, they just didn't lead to anyone.

Kaos frowned and took a step closer, his eyes full of compassion. "That sounds lonely."

Dylan danced around at the top of the stairs, reminding me I needed to get him bathed and to bed. "I gotta get him wound down," I said.

Kaos nodded. "There are four bedrooms on this floor. Check 'em out and pick one, Dylan."

Dylan shot off like a shot.

"No running in the house!" I shouted after him.

Shuffling his feet, he slowed his pace and slipped through a doorway. Hoping he wasn't getting into anything, I turned to face Kaos. "We shouldn't leave him alone."

"He's fine," Kaos said. "Nothing here will hurt him, and nothing's irreplaceable." He led me toward a door across the hall. "He's going to choose the room next door to this one. It was a second master, but I had it made into a kid's room. He'll love it. You can stay here, so you're close to him."

Like the rest of the house, the bedroom was tastefully decorated in grey, black, and white with a queen-sized bed, situated between two giant windows. We were on a hill, and the lights of Seattle shimmered below us. The day had been clear, and above, the rising moon was surrounded by twinkling stars. The entire view was stunning, and I found myself glued to it, wondering how I fit into this massive, intimidating world now. Despite the insanity that came afterward, Matt had been served divorce papers. Emily would file them in the morning, and in three months, I'd be free of him. I wondered where I'd go and what I'd do.

For the first time in a long time, I felt hopeful.

"This is amazing," I said. "Thank you."

He nodded. "You're welcome." I didn't take my gaze off the view, but I could see him out of the corner of my eye. He was watching me, much like I watched the view. I wondered what he saw. An abused woman trying to get her feet under her? A victim? Something more? No. I couldn't think about that right now. I pushed away from the wall.

Kaos was still watching me. He pointed toward a door. "Closet." To another door, he said, "Bathroom. Like I said, please, make yourself comfortable. If you need anything at all, there's a white board on the side of the fridge. My cousin will be here tomorrow. Carisa cleans and shops for me, and she'll pick up whatever you put on that board. I'm gonna tell Dylan goodnight, and then head upstairs. I have some calls to make, but if you need me, the staircase that leads to my room is at the end of the hall."

Knowing that this kind, beautiful man would be sleeping one floor up from me made my stomach feel strange again. I thanked him again and he stepped out of the room, giving me a moment alone before I had to track down my son and coax him into the bathtub. I collapsed on the bed and stared up at the ceiling, trying to make sense of how I felt.

Safe.

The word thrummed through me over and over like a prayer. Dylan and I were safe.

At least, for now.

9

Kaos

I COULDN'T STOP touching Tina. Her shoulder, her back, her arm, her neck, every inch of her body called to me like I was a goddamn kid again, and she was a new texture I had yet to discover. It started with an accidental brush of our arms, and before I knew it, I had my hand on the small of her back, relishing in the curve that flared out to her ass.

I liked touching her. It felt... right somehow. And the more I touched her, the harder it was to stop. I probably would have draped my arm over her shoulders, but that seemed a little too familiar. She was a mom with all the responsibilities that came with the title, and I needed to restrain myself and respect her role. The luggage had to be carried upstairs, so that kept my hands busy for a few minutes.

But then she stopped to study my family photos, and the fucking bone deep loneliness that emanated from her made me itch to drop everything and comfort her. Eyes soft with a sad smile ghosting her lips, she stared at the picture of my parents, talking about what had happened to her own. Her odd, estranged relationship with her uncle really threw me for a loop. I couldn't imagine living a life without family up in your business all the time.

All Tina had was Elenore and Dylan.

Yet she was so strong, so goddamn unbreakable. Life had heaped extra helpings of shit onto her shoulders, but she didn't give up. She was here, fighting for herself and Dylan, and I respected the hell out of her hustle.

She was wounded, but she was still in the game.

I wanted to call a time out so I could wrap my arms around her and shield her from the world.

Then, I wanted to kick myself for even considering such a thing.

She'd already had one asshole impose his will on her, she sure as shit didn't need another. Besides, I wasn't a shield; I was a center. I was all about that offense. My game plan included plays like breaking away from the defenders to score the game winning goal. Never in my life had I even considered hunkering down and protecting home. That sounded more like a goalie than anything.

Goalies had the hardest job on the ice—and I had every respect for them—but I'd never wanted to be one.

Yet here I was.

I studied the breathtaking woman before me, noting the pain and longing in her eyes even while her back was straight, her posture unyielding. The man who was supposed to be her teammate had turned on her. Life had shed its gloves and was going at her bare-fisted. Nobody would blame her one bit if she hunkered down and protected herself, but she wasn't that woman. She'd marched her determined ass into Ladies First and helped them come up with a plan to get back her freedom. She'd stayed in the game with only her sister and her son to support her.

"That sounds lonely," I said, trying to imagine a world without my crazy family. I couldn't. They were so ingrained in the very fabric of my being, I had no idea what my life would be like without them. I didn't even want to think about it.

I wanted to tell her how badass I thought she was, but Dylan kept bouncing off the walls, and she was distracted, needing to take care of him. Besides, she wasn't mine to lift up. She was still married. With a fucking kid.

The realization hit me like a sucker punch. Sure, she and her piece of shit husband had been separated for seven months and she'd filed for divorce, but still. Secretly lusting after her curvy body was one thing. Wanting to be a part of her life? That should feel wrong.

Right?

So why the fuck didn't it?

Shaking my head at my sudden willingness to break my moral code for this woman, I led her to her room. I intended to drop her ass off and get out of there, but the sight of her staring out at the city, looking so vulnerable and alone knocked me sideways. She tugged at impulses I didn't even know I had, making it almost impossible to keep my hands off her and walk out the goddamn door.

But she had enough going on without me planting myself in her life, demanding attention she didn't have to give. I needed to back off and let her figure shit out first. Maybe a little time and self-control would help me get past whatever the fuck kept tugging me toward her.

As fucked-up as it was, I wanted her in my bed.

A good old-fashioned ride on my cock would no doubt do wonders for her psyche. For a few hours, I could make her forget all about that abusive shitstain she'd married, and remind her of her own power as a gorgeous, sexual being. She deserved pleasure, passion, and release, and I could damn well give that all to her.

But what would happen afterward?

Tina didn't strike me as a fuck-and-forget-it woman. Even if she was, I couldn't imagine any mom having the luxury of no-strings-attached sex. If I somehow managed to get into her pants, the experience would no doubt be followed up by an awkwardness—and maybe even regret—that would make her feel unwelcome in my home.

No matter how much I wanted her, she and Dylan needed the safe haven I'd provided, and I refused to let my aching cock take away their security.

Still, it took everything in me to drag my ass away from her door.

When I finally did, I found Dylan exactly where I knew he'd be. Chuckling, I stepped into the room I'd had furnished and decorated for my nieces and nephews and shook my head. The kid had a virtual reality headset on and was standing in the center of the room waving the controllers wildly.

"Beat Saber?" I asked.

"Yep. I'm killin' it." He swung a few more times, stopped, and pushed the headset up to his forehead so he could see me. "You have the coolest shit, Kaos."

"Why thank you, but I don't think your mom would appreciate that language."

He dropped his gaze, frowning, and I could almost feel my upgraded status slipping away. "You use those words," he said.

I nodded. "I also pay my own bills. Regardless, you better believe I don't cuss in front of my mom."

"Why not?"

"It would upset her, and she's a good woman who's done a lot for me. I don't like to upset her. You see, the sum of who you are and what you do in life can be attributed to the people around you. Part of growing up is realizing who's helped you out and sacrificed to get you where you are in life. My dad worked a lot, so it fell on my mom's shoulders to get me to hockey practice. I'm sure she had other stuff she would have rather done, but she didn't miss a single game when I was growing up. I could always look up in the stands and see her cheering me on. Why would I want to disrespect someone who was always in my corner?"

He stared at me, his expression thoughtful. "That's a fair point, I suppose."

I bit back a laugh. "It's a damn good point. Now, time to put the game up for the night." I held out my hand and he reluctantly handed over the headset and controllers. I stashed them in the highest cabinet to dissuade him from trying to get them down. "You can play with the VR set again tomorrow. If you touch it before then, I'll take it away for a week. Understand?"

He nodded. Dylan was a smart kid who needed to know where the lines were drawn and what the consequences would be if he crossed them.

"Good. Follow the rules and we'll get along just fine. As you can tell, I like kids to have fun while they're in my house."

Dylan nodded again, his gaze taking in the three sets of bunk beds, the fifty-two-inch television with multiple game consoles attached, the bean bags, the chest of nerf guns and bullets, and the bookshelf stocked with handheld game machines and games. "It's weird that you don't have any kids," he said.

I chuckled. "Yeah. I like to go a little overboard when it comes to spoiling my nieces and nephews. They're good kids who work hard in school and I think that shit should be rewarded, you know?"

He dropped his gaze guiltily and gave me a shrug. "Yeah. I guess." He'd come around eventually. The kid just needed a little time and guidance.

"Did you bring soap and shampoo with you?" I asked.

His head snapped back up. "Yep."

"Get them out of your bag and I'll show you how to turn the bath on and off. You're old enough to do that, right?"

"Of course I am." Looking mildly offended, he marched over to one of his bags and unzipped it, searching through the contents until he retrieved two bottles.

"I figured as much," I said, leading him toward the attached bathroom. I pointed at a cupboard. "Grab yourself a towel and a washcloth out of there. If you run out of soap or shampoo, that's where I keep extras." Kneeling beside the bathtub, I pointed out the controls. "This activates the stopper to keep the water in." I flicked it up and down, demonstrating how it worked before turning on the water. "Left is hot, right is cold, toward the middle should be just right, but I'll let you figure out how warm you want it. You know your left from your right, don't you?"

The cocky little bastard dropped his shoulders and cocked his head to the side, looking like he was questioning my intelligence. "Everyone knows that."

I bit back a chuckle. "Oh yeah? Hold up your left hand."

He took a second to think about it, and then his left hand shot up.

"Good. I'll leave you to it, then. Your mom should be in any minute, but she's had a rough day so I'm hopin' you can give her a little bit of a break. I know you're a kid and it's in your nature to push back, but how about you wash yourself up and get to bed without giving her a hard time? Just for tonight?"

He frowned, but agreed, "Okay. I can do that."

"I know you can. Thanks, man." I clapped him on the shoulder as I stood. "I'm glad you guys are here. Get a good night's sleep, and I'll see you in the morning. As long as you don't get into trouble at school, we'll see if you're as good at air hockey as you are at foosball."

He grinned. As I turned to leave, he surprised me by saying, "Thanks, Kaos."

I gave him a manly nod of my head, encouraging his appreciation, but careful not to appear too enthusiastic about it. There was a fine line between the two, and it had to be carefully trod. "No problem."

Still fighting back a smile, I stepped into the bedroom and found Tina standing there. I had no idea how long she'd been listening in on my conversation with Dylan, but her eyes were glassy, and her hands were clasped in front of her. Curiosity raised her eyebrows as she looked at me like she was seeing me for the first time.

Unable to stop myself, I stepped closer until only inches separated us. Searching her face for clues about what was going on in her head, I asked, "Everything okay?"

"You didn't have to help him. I was coming. I just... needed a minute." The smile she gave me was... forced and unnatural, a complete contrast to the honesty we'd shared earlier.

I didn't like the way it twisted up my stomach. "I don't mind helping out. I like Dylan. He's a good kid. I'm sorry if I overstepped by showing him how to use the tub. The controls are simple, and I figured you could use a little break. You're not some kind of superhuman, and nobody here expects you to be."

"I..." She sucked down a shaky breath and looked away. "You didn't overstep, I'm not used to... I don't know what I'm trying to say. It *has* been a rough day. Thank you for starting his bath and for encouraging him to step up. That was... really thoughtful."

Her body seemed to lean toward me, and I couldn't tell if she was aware of it or not. Instinctively, I reached for her. My fingertips brushed her arm, but she sidestepped my hand and disappeared into the bathroom, closing the door behind her. I stared after her for a moment, wondering what the hell had just transpired between us. She had to feel our off-the-charts chemistry, but she was doing her damnedest to ignore it.

Tina was going through hell and she needed space and time. I could give her that. Resigned, I headed upstairs, pulling out my cell phone to call Link along the way. It was past time for me to check in, and I could obviously use the distraction.

"Hey Kaos, I was just about to call you," he said upon answering. "You get Tina and Dylan situated?"

I appreciated the way he referred to them by name. To the club, they weren't targets or jobs. They were people with real lives and individual identities. "Sure did, Prez. She's giving him a bath as we speak. I watched for a tail but didn't see shit. Did Matt ever show up at the condo?"

"No." Link hesitated. "Well, not to the condo. Morse was able to hack into the parking garage's camera feed and caught his vehicle making the rounds a few minutes after Tap drove her car out of there, but the son-of-a-bitch never parked or approached the building."

"Think he was lookin' for her car?"

"Makes sense. Let's hope the fucker comes lookin' for it here. Has Tina said anything about her plans for the week?"

I ambled through my bedroom door and sat on the corner of the bed. "She mentioned that Dylan has school, but I don't know if it's a good idea for him to go." Balancing my phone on my shoulder, I started tugging off my boots and socks.

"Not our call, I'm afraid. All we can do is make suggestions and be there to support whatever decisions she makes. We're not protective custody and she and her boy aren't our prisoners. Don't try to keep them from livin' their lives, but do what you can to protect them."

Right. Like taking candy from a toddler: tricky as hell and there was no way to come out of it without feeling like an asshole. "Any suggestions?"

"See if she'll let you play chauffeur. If that motherfucker is waiting at the school, you can keep her safe and make sure he doesn't follow her back to your place. If you need backup or assistance, call and we'll be there."

"Will do. How's her sister? Was Tap able to talk Elenore into letting him ramp up her security?"

Link chuckled. "Sure was. You'll learn Tap doesn't mince words or waste time. Most people appreciate that kind of honesty, and she was all over it. He replaced her locks, installed a camera over her door, loaded her up with a Taser and enough pepper spray to take down a goddamn bear, and got the hell out of there."

And from my brief encounter with Elenore, I'd bet she was

hoping for the opportunity to use that Taser and pepper spray on Matt. "Tina will be relieved to hear it," I said. "By the way, was everything okay with Matt's signature? Emily has everything she needs now, right?"

"Yeah." Link sounded surprised I'd asked. "She'll be filing the papers first thing in the morning."

The amount of relief his assurance gave me was startling. "Thank you."

"It's what we do. Keep your eyes and ears open and let us know if you need anything," Link said.

We disconnected, and I tugged off my clothes, tossing them into the hamper so Carisa wouldn't skin me alive when she came to clean tomorrow. It didn't matter how much I paid my cousin to keep up my house, she'd still kick my ass if I left her a mess. I could always fire her and hire someone else for the job, but then the rest of my family would show up on my front lawn with pitchforks and torches to remind me of who I was and where I came from.

Sometimes, having a huge, fully engaged, close-knit family wasn't all it was cracked up to be.

Turning on the shower, I stepped into the stream and flicked the setting to massage, thankful for the instant hot water heater my plumber brother had talked me into purchasing. I closed my eyes and ducked my head beneath the stream, enjoying the way it worked over my scalp as my thoughts drifted back to Tina. Hell, she was always in the back of my mind these days, tugging at my attention with her intense hazel eyes and plump lips. My cock instantly hardened at the memory of her in her room, framed by the stars above and the lights of the city below.

Dylan had to be finished with his bath by now. She'd probably tucked him in and returned to her own room. Now, what was she up to? Did she let her hair down? Did she remove her clothes and get dressed for bed? Or was she standing in her own en suite, staring at the soaking tub?

Now that image had potential.

Focusing my imagination, I could almost see her starting the water before tugging off her shirt and bra. The round soft breasts—that had been calling to me since the day I met her—would bounce free, and she'd let out a sigh of relief. She'd unfasten her jeans and slide them and her panties over her shapely hips and down her thick, sexy thighs. Stepping free, she'd slip into the warm water, letting it leech away her tension as she rested her head against the back of the tub and closed her eyes.

When she slid the soapy washcloth over the mouth-watering swell of her tits, I'd be on her mind. She'd wish it was my hands caressing her soft skin and gliding over her most sensitive areas.

Running my own washcloth over my chest and down my stomach to my aching hard cock, I imagined the way her breath would hitch at the contact. Cloth wrapped around myself, I pictured her leaving a trail of suds over the dips and curves of her body. Circling her peaked nipples, drifting down to her belly before flaring out over her hips and thighs. She'd let out a needy little moan as the washcloth slipped between her legs and found her swollen folds.

Fuck.

What I wouldn't do to be that piece of cloth as it dipped down to stroke her clit. Her head would roll back, and her eyes would dilate as she rubbed herself. Would she feel scandalous and naughty to be pleasuring herself beneath my roof?

My cock throbbed, dripping precum. Needing some sort of release, I slid my soapy washcloth over myself, stroking up and down. I wondered how Tina would stroke herself. Was she more of a soft circles gal? Or would she apply pressure and rock her fingers back and forth? Would she focus solely on her clit? Or would her fingers find their way inside her tight pussy? What would she feel like, core clenching around those fingers? Would she go slow at first, inching one finger in, and then adding a second? What kind of sounds would she make? How would she taste?

Not knowing was driving me insane!

I was so desperate to watch her come that I could practically smell her arousal mixed with mine. I'd let her get herself off, and then I'd pull her out of that tub and drop to my knees to lap up her sweetness. I'd savor every drop, playing with her clit until another round of pleasure wracked her body.

Then I'd bend her over and drive my cock so deep inside her she'd be every bit as fucked up as she made me feel.

God, I had it bad.

Squeezing myself, I imagined the walls of Tina's pussy pulsing around me. My balls drew up and the bottom of my spine tingled. Light exploded behind my eyes as milky white ropes of cum joined the stream of water, pulling a shout from somewhere deep inside me. Exhausted and boneless, I leaned against the side of the shower, struggling to recover as hot water continued to work over the muscles of my back.

Holy shit. What the fuck was that?

Just thinking about the woman had given me the best orgasm I'd had in years. Possibly ever. Getting inside her would most likely fuck me up for good, but it was a risk I was all too willing to take. Fucking desperate to take, even.

As soon as she was ready.

Only she was a single mom and not the fuck toy my imagination wanted her to be. I'd have to consider Dylan and the long-term ramifications of getting between her legs. Screwing with Tina involved commitment, and she wasn't even officially divorced yet.

So why the hell was she invading my every fucking thought?

Disgusted with myself I turned off the water and reached for a towel. The last thing she needed was me mucking up her already messy situation. It would be better for everyone if I kept my distance until she figured out her shit. Right. I'd already decided to do that. So, why the fuck did I have to keep reminding myself she was hands off?

Determined not to touch her, I dried off, put on a pair of basketball shorts, and crawled into bed. It was still early, but it had been a long-ass day and I was exhausted.

Besides, I was already getting hard again, and if I had any intention of staying away from Tina, I needed to take care of that situation. Apparently, I was in for a masturbation marathon. Wrapping my hand around my cock, I closed my eyes and thought of Tina's perfect plump lips pressed tight around me...

10

Tina

I SHOULD HAVE been worried about Matt, but it was thoughts of Kaos that kept me up all night. He wasn't like anyone I'd ever met, and his sweet conversation with Dylan played on repeat in my mind, making me hopeful for a better life once we were free of Matt.

I wondered if Kaos would still be single when I was ready to start dating again. Then, I questioned my intelligence and sanity for even thinking such thoughts. The last thing I should be worried about was another man. Hadn't I learned my lesson? It was past time to focus on taking care of Dylan and surviving the next three months.

"You're not some kind of superhuman, and nobody here expects you to be."

Kaos's words kept tumbling through my mind, making me feel all kinds of things. He was kind, but also wrong. Matt *had* expected perfection from me. I felt woefully inadequate more days than not, wearing his disappointment like a collar that always returned me to that address. After all, I came with a massive amount of baggage that nobody sane would want to take on.

But Kaos had reached for me.

I could still feel his phantom fingertips brushing over my skin, sprouting goosebumps in his wake. He might not expect perfection from me, but he had to have some expectations. Some requirements. Could I live up to those? Would I even want to try? Mind spinning in circles, I stared at the ceiling and tried like crazy to count sheep.

Around six a.m., I gave up on pretending to rest and padded downstairs, planning to thank our host for his hospitality by cooking everyone a healthy breakfast. Since I was practically dead on my feet, I needed caffeine, first, but the kitchen countertops were void of anything that looked like a coffee maker. A small, copper pot sat beside the stovetop. I picked it up, eyed it suspiciously, and sniffed it. It smelled like coffee, but I had no idea how to use it.

With no other obvious options for caffeinating, I turned my focus toward food. Slipping into the pantry, I turned on the light and was bombarded with shelves full of cereal.

Tons of cereal.

We're talking a grocery store aisle of cereal.

No rice, no beans, no flour, no sugar, just a handful of spices and every brand of cereal known to man.

Laughing to myself at the ridiculousness of it, I tried the fridge and found an unopened box of butter, half a gallon of milk, and some Chinese takeout that smelled like it was at the end of its lifecycle. Not much to work with. While Dylan would no doubt be thrilled about living off *Cap'n Crunch* and *Cookie Crisp*, if we planned to stay at Kaos's for any stretch of time, I'd need more options. I glanced at the whiteboard Kaos had mentioned, but quickly dismissed it. His cousin might shop for him, but I would buy my own groceries.

Needing to start a list, I searched for a pen and paper for a while before remembering that this was the twenty-first century and I had other options. Pulling out my borrowed phone, I found the notes app and started my list. The sound of footsteps drew my attention, and I looked up in time to watch Kaos round the corner.

I was not at all prepared for the sight.

Eyes dark, hair mussed, wearing only a pair of faded black sweats that hung low on his hips, he was a treasure trove of well-defined pecs, abs, and biceps. All out there, exposed, just begging for me to gawk at him. His chest held a spattering of dark hair, but it was the hair on his lower belly—the trail that led down past the waistband of his sweats—that had my absolute attention. That happiest of trails filled my mind with the kind of explicit images that required the clutching of pearls and a whole slew of Hail Marys.

If I wasn't careful, Kaos's body would send me straight to hell.

"Good mornin'," he said.

His voice rumbled through every inch of me. It also must have kick-started my brain because I realized where I was staring, and my gaze immediately snapped up to his face. Where it should have been all along. A smile played at the corners of his lips and I knew I'd been caught. Heat flooded my cheeks as I hurriedly looked away.

"Morning." My voice squeaked. Seriously squeaked! Embarrassment hovering dangerously close to mortification levels I could never recover from, I cleared my throat and tried again. "Mornin'. I would have made coffee, but uh…" I pointed at the little copper pot beside the stovetop. "I don't know how to use that."

He padded over to the counter, scooped up the little copper pot, and took it to the sink. "Have you ever had Greek coffee?"

"No."

"It's a lot like Turkish coffee." He rinsed the pot, filled it, and held it up. "This is a *briki*." He pronounced the word bree-kee. "You like sugar in your coffee?"

"Yes. And I've never had Turkish coffee, either."

"Well, you're in for a treat." Carrying the pot to the stovetop, he turned on the gas and added a couple measures of ground coffee before retrieving a canister of sugar from the cupboard above the stove.

Ahh. At least he had sugar. I made a mental note to check out that cupboard and see what other ingredients were stashed up there. He added sugar to the pot and stirred, giving me a nice view of his ripped back. I'd never cared about shoulder blades before, but Kaos's were quite the focal point. I had to force my gaze away so I could take in the rest of him. Broad shoulders tapered down to his waist. Two incredibly sexy indentations peeked out above his low waistband, and I had the overwhelming desire to touch them and see what they felt like.

And his ass... holy crap, how was it even possible to look that good in sweats?

"Medium low heat, stir it until the sugar dissolves and then stop," he said, pulling me out of my lusty thoughts. Giving the pot a few more hard stirs, he set the spoon aside and turned to face me. Attention on the phone in my hand he asked, "Is everything okay?"

"Yes." Having completely forgotten all about my task, I held up the cell awkwardly. "Just working on a grocery list."

"Did you forget?" He tugged the magnetic whiteboard off the side of the fridge and held it out toward me. "That's what this is for."

"I'm not gonna bug your cousin with my list when I'm perfectly capable of shopping for my own groceries."

His eyebrows rose. "Why not? That's what I pay her for."

"No, you pay her to shop for and clean up after you. It's not fair to bombard her with two additional people to take care of. Besides, I like shopping for myself. I've never had a car before. I used to have to order groceries online and Matt would pick them up on his way home from work." Mentioning my ex was a total buzz kill, and I could tell Kaos recognized the change in my emotions by the way his eyes narrowed. But I wanted him to understand why my freedom was so important to me. I couldn't be locked up in a house again. "It's nice to be able to do for myself again."

"Got it." He snapped the whiteboard back onto the fridge before turning off the burner. "See this foam?" he asked.

Curious, I stepped around the bar and joined him. Heat radiated from his body, and I tried to stay out of his aura, but it kept drawing me in. Besides, I needed to be close to make out the little bubbles that had formed on the top layer of the copper pot. "Uh-hunh."

"This is how you know when it's done." He brought down two small coffee cups and picked up the pot, angling it over the first cup. "Since the foam pours first, you split it between the cups before divvying up the coffee."

After following his own instructions, he handed me a cup. He held his out in a mock toast and sipped. I followed suit. Bitter, sweet, strong, it was like condensed coffee.

"Mm. It's good. Thank you."

"No problem. Be sure to sip. There's grounds in the bottom, so don't go crazy and throw it back like a shot or you'll end up with a mouthful." His gaze dropped to my mouth and heat flared in his dark eyes. My stomach tightened as the air between us practically crackled with tension.

"Dylan," I blurted out, setting my cup down as my mom responsibilities kicked into overdrive. "I need to get him up and dressed so he can eat."

Before Kaos could respond, I dashed toward the stairs.

Dylan was still sound asleep and did not appreciate my interference, but I managed to get him up and dressed by tempting him with Kaos's cereal selection. By the time we reached the kitchen, Kaos had donned a T-shirt and was seated at the bar with his hands wrapped around his coffee cup. He greeted Dylan as we marched by, and I opened the pantry to prove to my son that I hadn't been exaggerating.

"Wow," Dylan said, taking in the shelves. He selected *Trix*, and I poured him a bowl while he climbed up on the stool beside Kaos.

"Want some?" I asked our host, holding up the box.

He nodded. "Please."

I plopped two full bowls down on the bar and Kaos thanked me. Then he elbowed Dylan in the side.

"Yeah, thanks, Mom," Dylan hurried to say.

Kaos smiled and launched into after school plans with my son while I sipped my coffee and tried to wonder if I should worry about the two of them getting so close. As far as men went, there were definitely worse ones out there for my kid to get attached to. Still, I had no idea how long we'd be staying with him, and Dylan's attitude, grades, and personality in general had already suffered enough when we'd left his father.

And Matt hadn't even paid much attention to him.

After a brief debate about the benefits of Kaos chauffeuring me to drop Dylan off at school—versus the risks of me doing it myself to protect my independence—I caved. My son's safety had to come above all else, and if Matt showed up, Kaos was a lot better equipped to handle him than I was. Dylan chatted the entire drive there, but the ride back to the house was quiet. The atmosphere wasn't necessarily uncomfortable, more like… charged. At one point, Kaos changed the radio station and his hand reached over and hovered above my leg. I expected him to touch me, but he didn't. Instead, he yanked his hand back and ran it through his hair looking flustered.

"I… I have to take the Jetta back to the club and get my bike," he said, his attention focused on the road ahead. "I'll drop you off at the house. You'll have the Escalade if you need to go anywhere, but I'll be back in plenty of time to take you to pick up Dylan. We can hit the grocery store afterwards, if you'd like."

I could find my way to the grocery store alone, but the way he was careful to let me know I wouldn't be trapped alone at his house did something to my chest. He cared enough to make sure I kept my freedom. Swallowing past the lump in my throat, I nodded. "Thank you."

When we got back to the house, Kaos showed me how to work the alarm system before hanging up the keys to the Escalade and taking off. I stared at the door for a few minutes—silently willing him to come back for reasons I wasn't ready to admit—before heading into the kitchen to finish my grocery list. All the while, I couldn't stop thinking about the man's bare chest, muscular back, and low-hanging sweatpants. My head was a mess, and I decided to distract myself by exploring.

The French doors off the dining room led to the most enchanting, peaceful backyard I'd ever seen. It was like some hidden forest paradise of greenery and stone. I stepped out onto the stone patio and took in the built-in stainless steel grill, with a countertop and a mini fridge. Two sets of patio furniture—each clustered around a fire pit—and a matching teak dining set for ten were situated around the grill. Beyond the stone patio, the grass landscape was broken up with sections of colorful trees, shrubs, bushes, ivy, and flowers. A shallow pond stocked with colorful koi wound around the vegetation. I followed it to the side of the house where it ended before reaching a connected stone waterfall.

A wooden bench sat on the other side of the waterfall. I settled onto the bench, leaned back, and closed my eyes. The day was cool, but the sun had breached the scattered clouds and beat down on me, sapping my strength. The clean smells, soft sounds, and safety of the secluded backyard lulled me into relaxing.

I must have drifted off to sleep, because a feminine voice pulled me out of my thoughts. "Dari— Oh. You are... not my cousin," she said.

I opened my eyes to find a gorgeous, dark-haired woman staring at me. Hurrying to my feet, I winced as a kink tugged at my neck and shuffled forward. "No. I'm Tina. I'm... um... staying with Kaos... with Darius for a little while."

"You're *staying* here?" Her eyebrows shot up. "Like... sleeping here?"

Unsure of how to take the disbelief that was written all over her face, I nodded. "Yes. Is... Is something wrong with that?"

"No. It's just surprising." She folded her arms across her chest and studied me. "He never has women here, so you two must be pretty serious."

"It's not like that," I rushed to say. "I was in a bind and he's helping me out. We're... friends." Friends seemed like a strange title to put on our relationship, since I'd only known him a couple of days, but I had no idea what else to call it.

"Ah. Okay, that makes more sense." Her shoulders relaxed. "Sorry, I'm Carisa, and you quite possibly just saved my life."

"I did?" I asked, confused.

She nodded. "If Darius was seeing someone and hadn't told Aunt Linore there'd be hell to pay and I'd have a very difficult choice to make. I could call and tattle, or, I could blackmail my cousin into all kinds of shit for keeping his secret. I most definitely would have settled on the latter. Then my aunt would have been murderous when she inevitably found out that I knew and hadn't immediately filled her in." She flashed me a smile. "So, thanks for keeping me from that suicidal decision."

She was quick-witted and charming, and I couldn't help but smile back at her. "My pleasure."

"But I do reserve the right to make said suicidal decisions in the future, so if the two of you do start dating, please be sure to let me know as soon as possible."

"I will," I promised. "But you're safe. I just escaped from a bad relationship and have no desire to hop right into another." Realizing how bad that sounded, I winced. "Not like a relationship with your cousin would be bad. That's not what I meant."

She laughed. Her gaze shot to my neck. She had to see the bruises, but thankfully, she didn't say anything about them. Instead, she gave me a reassuring smile. "I think you and I are going to get along just fine. Come in and keep me company while I clean, will ya? I rarely have anyone other than family to talk to these days, and they're all so freaking boring they make me want to melt my eardrums."

That sounded serious, and like a fate I wanted to keep her from, so I followed her inside and went to the fridge like I owned the place. "Can I get you anything to drink? We have milk or... water."

She quirked an eyebrow at me.

"Sorry. Habit. I... Um..."

Laughing, she went to the cupboard and pulled down two wine glasses. Opening a second cupboard, she paused. "Dammit. I must have drunk all the good stuff last time I was here. You wanna hit the store?"

"Yes!" I practically jumped at the invitation. "I made a list this morning."

"For the love of God, please tell me there's more on it than cereal," she said.

We took the Escalade because Carisa said it made her feel bougie to drive it. I was just glad she wanted to drive, because it looked like a beast to park. Shopping with her was an experiment in people-watching and trash-talking that had me laughing harder than I had in ages. But, as we rolled up to the checkout, I pulled out my credit card and fun time ended.

"What the hell do you think you're doing?" she asked, sounding offended.

"Paying," I replied, voicing the obvious.

"Nope. Put that thing away before you hurt your bank account. Darius has this."

"I want to help," I insisted.

"Then cook for him. You'll save him a fortune in food delivery."

"I'd be buying groceries for me and Dylan wherever we stayed," I said.

Her eyebrows rose. "Dylan?"

"My son." I was surprised he hadn't come up yet, but we hadn't really talked about our families.

"Then you're definitely not paying. There's at least three-hundred-dollars worth of wine in that cart. It's part of the deal I made with Darius. I clean and shop, and he splurges on the good wine."

"Three-hundred-dollars? In wine?" I swallowed, barely stopping myself before I put a hand to my chest to make sure my heart was still beating. I couldn't even wrap my mind around spending so much money on alcohol.

She grinned. "It should hold us over until Friday when I go grocery shopping again."

I was out of my depth, dealing with people who clearly had a different relationship with money than I did. Backing off, I let Carisa pay for the groceries. Then we loaded them up and drove back to the house where she opened a bottle of the crazy expensive wine and threatened me until I accepted a glass. I justified it by helping her clean. We washed windows and chatted. I avoided the topic of Matt, but I did tell her all about my son.

"What about you?" I asked. "You have any kids?"

"No." Sadness filled her eyes before she looked away. "I was married once, though. Bryan was a good man. We wanted to start a family, but he died before we could get pregnant."

"I'm sorry," I said. "What happened?"

"Inoperable brain tumor. We'd only been married a few months when they found it."

She sounded so sterile, like a doctor delivering a diagnosis. My heart went out to her, but I had no idea what to say.

"At the time, I was working a stressful job at a big insurance company, and I couldn't keep it together. But I had bills, and Bry's life insurance didn't go nearly far enough to cover them. I had to sell my house. Darius offered to buy it, but I couldn't... Bry and I had purchased it together and everything about it reminded me of him. I couldn't keep it. Darius let me move in here and he fired his cleaning lady to give me a job. I lived here and kept the place up for him while he was in the service."

"He really is a nice guy, isn't he?" I asked.

"He's the best. I don't know what I would have done without him. It's been five years since I lost Bry, and my family thinks it's time for me to move on. They keep trying to set me up. This place is my escape," she explained. "Like a little oasis of wine and cleaning products."

After the windows, we started laundry and I swept the downstairs while she dusted. We had just met back up to tackle the downstairs bathroom when Kaos appeared in the doorway with a food bag in hand. He was wearing the same black leather vest over a fitted white T-shirt, jeans, and boots he'd left in. My gaze was immediately drawn to the way his short sleeves hugged his muscular biceps. He had great forearms, too. They flexed as he held up the bag and asked, "You two feel like takin' a break?"

Heat blossomed in my cheeks when I realized I was staring—and possibly drooling—and I dropped my gaze.

Beside me, Carisa shifted, dropping her sponge into the tub. "Absolutely." She grabbed my arm and held me back for a moment as Kaos walked away. "You didn't tell me it was like that," she whispered.

More heat blazed in my cheeks. "Like what?"

She chortled, and the devious gleam in her eyes set me on edge. "Oh, this is gonna be fun."

Pretending I didn't have the first clue what she was talking about, and failing miserably, I let her tug me along as she followed Kaos into the kitchen. He sat at the end of the bar, and Carisa planted herself two stools down, gesturing for me to sit between them. Bad idea. Very bad idea. That would put me entirely too close to the man for comfort, and I had no idea how my body would react. My brain screamed at me to abort mission and flee from the room, but I didn't want to look like a raving lunatic. I probably wouldn't even think about the last time we were together in his kitchen, while he was bare-chested with that tantalizing happy trail leading down to...

No!

Locking down those dangerous thoughts, I squeezed in beside him, brushing against his arm. Gritting my teeth, I ignored the sparks that erupted at the contact. Butterflies did gymnastics in my stomach, but I couldn't be bothered with those, either. I scooted away from him, as far as the seat would allow. My entire body revolted at the sudden distance between us, and I had to force myself not to lean against him. Posture so rigid I probably looked like there was a stick up my butt, I fought to maintain control.

Kaos handed me a gyro. Our fingertips brushed, and I didn't know whether to grab his hand or to wipe the memory of his touch off on my leggings. I settled for wrapping both my hands securely around the sandwich in a death grip so I wouldn't lose my mind and do something stupid.

Like straddle him.

Straddling him would feel so good.

And it would be so bad.

Carisa was watching me. I could feel her gaze burning a hole in the side of my head, but I refused to look at her. She was already onto me, and the fire raging in my cheeks had to be giving her all the confirmation she needed. Thankfully, she leaned forward and looked past me, "Where have you been all day, cuz?"

"The club. What have you two been up to? Besides drinking up all my wine." He gestured toward the empty bottle on the counter.

"We went grocery shopping," Carisa said. "For actual groceries. Turns out your girl here can cook and is willing to use her culinary skills on you."

"We're just friends," I said at the same time Kaos asked me, "You wanna cook?"

"Friends," I said again, unsure of why I felt it necessary to repeat myself. "And yes, cooking is the least I can do. You're letting us stay here."

He held my gaze, and I got the feeling he was searching for something in my eyes, but I had no idea what. "You don't have to do that," he said. "Or anything. Bad enough that Carisa has you doin' her job. You're guests."

Carisa snorted. "As if I could stop her."

"I like to cook," I said.

He gave me a lopsided smile. "Well, I like to eat, so..." Unwrapping his gyro, he took a bite.

His mouth was fascinating. Full lips surrounded by a well-groomed mustache and goatee. Stubble dusted his jaw and the lower half of his cheeks. He swallowed and his Adam's Apple bobbed up and down.

"That's settled then," Carisa said.

I practically jumped out of my skin but recovered by pushing out of my seat—this time, toward Carisa—and leaping halfway across the kitchen.

"You okay there, Tina?" Carisa asked with far too much laughter in her voice.

Nodding, I opened a cupboard. "Yep. Just thirsty." Quite the understatement, since my throat felt like the Sahara Desert. "You want anything to drink?"

She picked up the second bottle of wine she'd opened and poured the last of it into her glass. "Nope. I'm good, thanks."

"Kaos?" I asked, trying not to look at him.

Carisa leaned forward, settling her elbow on the bar and using her hand to prop up her head as she stared at her cousin. "Yeah, *Kaos*, are you thirsty, too? Or is it just our friend Tina, there?"

I liked Carisa, but I was going to have to kill her.

"A glass of water would be great," he replied. "And don't mind my cousin. She treats wine like it's a food group, and it makes her a little bonkers."

Carisa rolled her eyes. "Grapes *are* fruit. It's science."

I filled two water glasses and plunked them down on the bar before circling back around to retake my seat. Unwrapping my gyro,

I bit into it. The flavor was excellent, but my stomach was far too active for such nonsense and wanted nothing to do with food. Forcing down the bite, I reached for my glass and guzzled down the water. When I came up for air, both Kaos and Carisa were staring at me.

Calmly rewrapping my sandwich, I stood. "I'm gonna... I'm not all that hungry, so I'll just put this away for later and get back to the bathroom."

Before either of them could respond, I stashed my sandwich in the fridge and fled up the stairs. Halfway up, I remembered we'd left off in the downstairs bathroom. Too bad. I'd just have to settle for starting on Dylan's bathroom instead, because there was no way in hell I was going back down those stairs.

I was busily scrubbing down the tub when Carisa joined me. She popped out a hip to lean against the sink, folding her arms as she watched me work.

"I like you, Tina," she said. "I've decided you can date my cousin, but," I started to object, but she held out her hand to stop me. "Don't even try to deny your attraction. I was just in the kitchen with the two of you, and whew. Girl, if contact pregnancy ever becomes a thing, the vibes you two are throwing up could populate a freaking country. But that's all fine as long as you don't try to take away my job. I've got a good thing going here. I always knew Darius would hit it big, and I put in the time to ensure my spot as his favorite cousin. Nothin' personal, but if you try to take this from me, I will smash a wine bottle and use it to rip out your jugular. Know that in your heart."

That sounded pretty dang personal to me, but I held up my hands in surrender. "I would never take your job away from you." I dropped my scrubber and sat on the edge of the bathtub so I could face her. "But you have nothing to worry about, because nothing can happen between me and Darius. Not for several months, at least. I need to get my life together first and figure out what I want to do."

"Oh, honey." Her eyes softened and she let out a little giggle. "You think you can control emotions? That's so... adorable. Naive, but adorable."

"I'm serious."

"I know you are, which makes it even better."

I kind of wanted to shake her. "Nothing is going to happen."

She laughed, throwing her head back and everything. When she finally regained control, she wiped away tears from beneath her eyes and held up her wine glass in a mock toast. "To bullshit declarations of abstinence. This really is gonna be fun."

11

Kaos

THE MOMENT TINA fled out of earshot, Carisa turned on me, gesturing wildly at the now vacant stool between us. "What the actual fuck was that?" she asked.

The "that" in question, had been one hell of a sexually charged lunch. Tina had been blushing and stammering, and every muscle in my body was sore from the strain of not reaching for her. Of not wrapping my arms around her and burying my face in her neck. If my cousin hadn't been there, things between Tina and me probably would have escalated until I stripped her bare, sat her ass on the countertop, and fucked her right there in my kitchen.

And then afterward, there would have been hell to pay.

But since I couldn't say any of that without sounding like I was out of my fucking mind, I decided to be a smartass. Gaze snapping to the stool, I replied, "*That* was once a tree. Though technically, it started out life as a seed. Which begs the question... what came first, the seed or the tree? I'd say the answer depends on whether you believe in creation or evolution."

She blinked. "Are you for real right now?"

I shrugged. "Dunno. Are any of us really real?" She was making this too damn easy. "I could be a figment of your imagination. This entire universe could be just a program aliens are running in your head while you're plugged into their matrix. Who knows? Maybe your drunk ass slipped and bashed in your noggin, and now you're stuck in your own mind."

Her expression flattened. "I'm talking about the fireworks going off between you and Tina." Carisa narrowed her eyes at me. "Have you guys... hooked up yet?"

Hooked up? What were we? Teenagers? I shook my head. "It's not like that. She's going through a messy divorce. Her ex is a piece of shit, and I'm putting her up until she can get free of him."

Carisa continued to study me. "She said she has a kid."

"Dylan." I fought a smile at the mention of the boy. "He's a quick-witted little asshole who likes to put me in my place. You'll love him."

Her expression went all soft. "That is adorable," she said, pointing at me.

"What?"

"That thing your face does when you talk about him. You called him an asshole, but you like the kid."

"He *is* an asshole," I defended. "Way too smart for his own good, but he's also a great kid."

"I don't doubt it." She pushed the rest of her sandwich aside and took another sip of wine. "I like Tina. She's... she's a good person. She has a work ethic and morals and shit. Insisted on helping me even though I tried to explain that this is my job. The woman isn't looking for a free ride. When we went grocery shopping, I thought I was going to have to throw down to keep her from paying. Luckily, I snagged a few bottles of wine I figured were well out of her price range. She had no choice but to let me flash your credit card."

I grinned. "That's dirty." And I was glad Carisa had done it.

Since Tina wasn't working, she needed to keep whatever money she had.

"Sure is." Carisa sounded proud of herself. "Tina's a little uptight, but I'm betting that has to do with her ex. It's clear there's sparks pingin' between you two, so what's the problem? Why haven't you made a move?"

"One does not make moves on single moms." I finished off my water and stood, taking my wrapper to the trash.

Sliding her elbows onto the counter, she laced her fingers, plopped her chin on top of them, and stared at me. "Why? You don't think single moms need love, too?"

It felt like a loaded question. Wondering what kind of trap she was setting for me, I replied, "Single moms don't need casual."

"Oh." Her nod was exaggerated. "So, you're an expert on the sexual needs of women. I get it now. Please... mansplain away to me."

Yep. I'd walked right into that one. "That's not what I mean."

"Good, because I'd imagine being a single mom would be really lonely. Having a kid doesn't magically erase a woman's desire to be wanted. It doesn't rip away her sex drive. Besides, who says it has to be casual? You like her and her kid. If things go well between the sheets, this could be an actual relationship."

There was no universe in which I wanted to discuss sex drives and relationships with my cousin. I needed to turn this ship around. Quickly. "I've only known her about five minutes."

"Yet she and her son are staying here," she fired back. "In your house."

"They had nowhere else to go."

She eyed me. "King County has more than ten-thousand homeless people." She swirled the remaining swallow of wine around in her glass before downing it. "Bet some are moms with kids who are also out of options. Strange how you never brought any of them home."

I let out a sigh. "It's complicated."

"Yep. Relationships always are." She rose, wrapped the rest of her gyro up and put it in the fridge.

"He beat her," I said, hating the way the words tasted in my mouth.

Carisa spun around, her brow furrowed in concern. "The bruises... on her neck. He did that?"

I nodded. "But that's nuthin.' I saw pictures. The fucker did a lot worse. It was bad. Really fuckin' bad."

She closed the fridge, leaning against the door, and let out a breath. "Well, shit. You're probably right to take things slow then."

My eyebrows shot up. "I'm right?" None of the women in my family had ever made such a crazy announcement. "That's a first. Shouldn't there be balloons and streamers and shit?"

Her eyes narrowed. "Let's not get crazy, I said *probably* right. Only time will tell." She moseyed over to the sink, rinsed out her wine glass, and set it in the dishwasher. Pushing off the counter, she headed toward the living room like our conversation was over. But as she reached the doorway, she spun around to frown at me thoughtfully. "You're a good man, cuz. One of the best I've ever known."

Carisa and I gave each other non-stop shit. I was used to her throwing insults or backhanded compliments my way, so I waited for the other shoe to drop.

"Be careful. Hurt people can really *hurt* people," she said, her eyebrows dropping in thought. "But don't forget that healed people can also *heal* people. You've gotten over a lot of shit in your lifetime. If I live to be a hundred, I swear I'll never understand your reason for joining the military—and then a biker gang—but it's clear it was all part of your healing process. You're less... self-absorbed now."

"A biker club," I corrected. "And gee, thanks."

She snorted. "Whatever. Regardless, you're still far from perfect, but who knows? Maybe the shit you've been through uniquely qualifies you to help Tina and Dylan out."

I frowned, letting her words sink in. "Like a friend."

"Sure." She shrugged. "If that's what you need to tell yourself. But I have a feeling the first time you two are alone, things are gonna get really freaky around here."

Out of principle, I wanted to argue, but before I could even call bullshit, she turned and walked out. Besides, as much as I hated to admit it, she was right. There were fireworks between me and Tina. The timing was shit, which meant I needed to make sure Tina and I were never alone so the sparks between us wouldn't have the chance to catch us both ablaze. I saw a lot of quality time with my hand in the near future. At least Tina's sexy-ass curves and shy smile would provide plenty of material for my spank bank.

Maybe someday I'd get the opportunity to see how red I could make her cheeks.

Eventually.

When she wasn't in the middle of a messy divorce.

Fuck.

Yep. My right hand would be getting some major action in the days to come. I'd have to start doing extra curls on my left side, so I didn't end up with one Popeye forearm. Shaking my head at myself, I set my glass in the dishwasher and headed upstairs. I had time to tie one off before we had to leave to pick up Dylan.

Over the rest of the week, Tina, Dylan, and I fell into a comfortable routine. In the mornings, she'd make breakfast. The three of us would eat together at the bar, and then we'd take Dylan to school. Afterwards, I'd drop her fine ass and the Escalade off at the house, hop on my bike, and put some distance between us. I could never tell if Tina was disappointed or relieved to see me go. Usually, I went to the fire station. There, I hung around like a lump on a log—trying to make myself useful but with nothing to do—until about an hour before Dylan got out of school. Then,

I'd come home, pick her up, and we'd go retrieve the kid together.

We didn't exactly avoid each other; we just limited our alone time.

The minutes we did spend together were pure fucking torture.

Whenever she so much as crossed her legs or shifted her stance, my body reacted. With every shy smile and averted gaze, my cock hardened. Her scent lingered in pockets of my house, driving me out of my mind. I wanted her so damn bad that not even my hand could satisfy me anymore. Most nights, I could barely get it out of my mind that she was only a floor beneath me, lying in bed, probably every bit as hot and bothered as I was. Hard as a rock, I tossed and turned until I finally passed out.

I had no idea how long we could share a roof before I snapped and broke down her fucking bedroom door.

I made it to Thursday before Tap took one look at me, ushered me into the office he shared with Morse and Hound, and said, "The club's still an option. If Tina and Dylan are too much, they can stay here."

Knowing I looked like shit, I ran a hand over my face, trying to wipe away the exhaustion. "Any sign of Matt?"

"Nope," Tap replied. "The bastard hasn't shown up at Elenore's either. Don't expect him to as long as we keep Tina's car and cell phone here."

"You think he tracked them here?" I asked.

Morse popped his head up from behind his monitor. "He graduated cum laude from UDub and works in software development. He's a smart, tech-minded son-of-a-bitch. I'd bet Hound's left nut that he at least tracked her phone here."

UDub was what the locals called the University of Washington. Back when I'd been looking at colleges, UDub required a 3.8 GPA and only had about a fifty percent acceptance rate. Unless things had drastically changed, it was one hell of a hard school to get into. Matt had to be book smart at least.

"What the fuck, man?" Hound asked, spinning around to face us. "Bet your own damn balls. I have plans for mine."

"He proposed to Mila last night," Morse said.

Nodding, Hound grinned. "She said yes, by the way. Morse has been flickin' me shit ever since."

"Get used to it asswipe," Morse said. "We'll be family soon."

Mila was Morse's cousin. Because the club was full of gossips, I'd heard snippets about her fucked-up past. Hound's past wasn't much better, and his time in the Navy had left him disabled and in constant pain. They were good people who'd overcome a lot of obstacles and seemed genuinely happy together.

"That's great to hear." I stepped over to shake his hand. "Congrats, brother."

His grin widened. "Thanks, man."

"You guys planning a big wedding?" I asked.

"Fuck yeah, they will be," Morse said. "A club wedding. You haven't seen one of those yet, prospect, but you should start preparing your liver now. Tina and Dylan could go back to Elenore's. Rabbit's been spending plenty of time there. I'm sure he'll keep an eye on them."

That was news to me. "He is? Why?" I asked.

"None of our business," Tap said, giving Morse a pointed look.

"All I'm saying is that I've never known Rabbit to take vacation before, but he's been out all we—"

"None of our *fucking* business," Tap repeated.

Okay then. Something was clearly up. I looked to Morse, hoping to glean more information, but he was back to typing away and didn't pay me any mind.

I had so many questions.

But even if Morse was right and Rabbit was hanging out at Elenore's, he would have to go back to work eventually. So would Elenore. That would leave Tina and Dylan alone at the condo. Not an option.

Truth be told, even if Rabbit quit his job and spent every

moment of his life at Elenore's, I wouldn't want Tina and Dylan to move out of my house. Despite the torture of being so close to something I wanted but couldn't have, I enjoyed their company. Every evening, after we picked Dylan up from school, I helped him with his homework while Tina made dinner. Then the three of us played games or watched a movie together. It was a nice, easy, comfortable companionship I could definitely get used to. I didn't realize how lonely I'd been before they appeared, but now, I couldn't imagine my house without them in it.

"They're safer with me," I said.

Morse snorted.

Tap smirked but didn't say shit.

The look Hound gave me made it clear I hadn't fooled him, either.

Having voiced everything I planned to say on the matter, I got the hell out of there.

Saturday morning, Dylan and I had plans. Since I didn't want Tina to get cabin fever and go all *The Shining* on me, I arranged for her to get out of the house and have some fun, as well. Just not with me. I wasn't a fucking masochist, after all.

"Are you sure it's safe?" Tina asked, her hands resting protectively on Dylan's shoulders as worry drew lines across her forehead.

"I won't let anything happen to him," I assured her.

"It's safe," Dylan assured her. "Lots of kids play hockey, Mom. It would be illegal if it wasn't safe."

There were serious flaws in the kid's logic, but I didn't point them out. Thankfully, neither did Tina. Squeezing her eyes shut, she dropped a kiss on his forehead and released him. He leapt out of her reach like the ref had just released him from the penalty box and he was anxious to get back in the action.

"Be careful," Tina said.

"Have fun with Carisa, and don't worry about a thing." My cousin would be there any minute to take Tina out for a spa day. I didn't even want to know what the fuck that entailed, but it had been Carisa's idea.

Dylan and I hurried out the door before his mom could change her mind. He spent the entire drive firing off questions about the sport and talking about how great he was going to be at it. Judging by his enthusiasm, he fully expected to become some kind of hockey prodigy and get drafted into the NHL before finishing grade school. I did my best to ground him in reality without crushing his dreams, but the kid was a goddamn force.

"It's a lot of work," I said, parking in front of my buddy's rink.

"But you did it," he countered.

"Not until after college, and I worked my ass off to get in. Dylan, nothing in this life worth doin' is easy. The more work you put in, the greater the rewards."

He stared at me, cocking his head to the side as he opened his door. "You sound like my PE teacher."

"You already have physical education?" I got out of the Escalade and rounded the vehicle to help him out. Without waiting for me, he hopped down on his own, shutting the door behind him. "You're in like... what, second grade?"

He huffed. "Third."

"You like PE?"

He shrugged and followed me toward the front door. "It's better than reading, but Mr. White likes to talk too much. Sometimes he says stupid things and I get in trouble for pointing out how stupid they are."

This kid. So matter of fact about dressing down the adults in his life. Careful to keep my expression neutral, I said, "Yeah? Well, you gotta show adults respect."

"Why?"

I thought about it for a beat. "Because karma is real and growing up isn't easy. You go through a lot of shit and it either breaks you or makes you tough and wise. You'll be an adult someday, and after struggling through life to get there, you won't appreciate some punk-ass little kid calling you stupid."

Frowning, he looked down at his feet. "Yeah, but I'm not gonna say stupid shit when I'm a grown up."

I chuckled at his candor. "Okay, I'm gonna need an example. What did Mr. White say that has you all up in arms?"

"He made us run, and I was tired, so I started walking instead. He told me not to quit. He said I had to take quit and put it in my pocket." Dylan's face scrunched up with disgust as he gestured wildly. "I was wearing gym shorts. They don't even have pockets."

I could practically see the scene between Dylan and his teacher playing out in my head, and it was all I could do to keep from laughing. Most of the PE teachers I'd met were wannabe coaches who listened to too many motivational speakers and took themselves too seriously. "I take it you told him as much."

Dylan nodded. "And he sent a pink note home and I got in trouble. *He* said something stupid, and *I* couldn't play video games for a week. It wasn't fair."

The kid had a point.

We'd reached the door, but I stopped and turned to face him. "I'm gonna tell you something I wish someone would have told me when I was your age."

"Is it that life isn't fair?" he asked, his eyes full of barely suppressed pain. "Because my parents are getting a divorce, so I already know that."

Damn. That hit hard. Wishing I could take some of that hurt away from him, I shook my head. "No. I was going to tell you you're right, but it doesn't matter. Not one bit. The world doesn't care if you're right; they just want you to follow the rules. Society likes robots who do what they're told, but you're a free thinker. So, you need to be okay with knowing you're right in your heart, while pretending to play by their rules. Then life will be easier for you."

He stared at me, his forehead scrunching up. "What do you mean?"

"Well, life's a lot like hockey," I said, leaning against the building. "If you put a bunch of guys on the ice with sticks and told them to score points, it would be chaos. You'd get the same result if you set kids loose without guidelines and let them do their own thing. Rules were created to keep everything civil. On the ice, refs make sure everyone follows the rules. In life, the people enforcing the rules change based on where you are and what you're doing. As a kid, your parents, teachers, and other adults keep you in line and punish you when you step out. They're like the refs in your life."

He folded his arms across his chest. "But sometimes they're wrong."

I chuckled. "They sure are. You think refs are always right? They're not. They make bad calls. Like everyone else, they're only human. The majority are good people who do their best to make fair calls and not show favoritism to one team or another. Don't get me wrong, there are some dirty assholes in the bunch, but for the most part, they're just trying to do their job. Adults are no different."

He stared at me thoughtfully.

"But... here's where it gets tricky. Say you're out on the ice and a ref makes a bad call. What do you think will happen if you call him stupid?"

"I don't know."

"He'll boot your ass out of the game. You gotta be strong enough to know you're right, and smart enough to keep your mouth shut about it."

"If a ref makes a bad call, someone should tell him."

I nodded. "Sure, but it won't matter. The only way a ref's gonna change his mind, is if he sees something on the instant replay. Average, ordinary people don't have that option. Besides, what difference do you think it'll make? Your teacher wasn't trying to be stupid. He was trying to inspire you to be better. You can't fight everything you don't agree with, Dylan. You do that, you'll become the problem. Trust me, you don't want to be that guy."

He stared at me. I got the feeling he wanted to argue, but he held his tongue and mulled over my words. Hell, I could practically see the wheels spinning in his head. Little by little, I was getting through to the kid. Knowing my words had an impact felt like a fucking bear hug straight to my heart. Shaking off the warmth before it got uncomfortable, I swung open the door.

"Come on. Let's get you into a pair of skates and see how you do on the ice."

As anticipated, it took a little time for Dylan to get his feet under him, but once he managed to find his balance, he was a fearless little terror. I watched him go full-bore into the boards, bounce off, and then do it again without a moment of hesitation. We did nothing but skate that first day, and by the end of it, he was dragging ass and still begging me to stay longer.

"You have to be hungry," I said. Hell, I was starving, and I hadn't worked half as hard as the kid. "Let's pick up something to eat and head home."

"Fine." His shoulders slumped. "But we didn't even play any hockey."

"We will," I assured him.

"Tomorrow?"

I laughed. "You're gonna be sore tomorrow. We'll probably have to give it a little while. I'll reach out to my buddy and see when the ice is open next. Maybe we can get you into some classes. In the meantime, I'm gonna order a couple of books. I want you to read over the rules of the game and learn the language. Can't have you making me look bad in front of the other kids."

"I'm gonna have to read? And learn new words?"

"I think you'll live." I led him to the bench where we removed our skates. "Your mom said your grades have been slipping, but you're probably the smartest third grader I've ever met. What's goin' on with that?" I asked.

Following me toward the locker room, he said, "I've had a lot goin' on, Kaos."

He sure had, but it was an excuse that could easily become a crutch. "So?"

He frowned. "I'm not perfect, okay?"

I bit back a laugh. "Nobody expects you to be, buddy. You ever hear of Socrates?"

Dylan shook his head.

"He was a great Greek philosopher who said, 'The secret of change is to focus all your energy, not on the fighting of the old, but the building of the new.' You understand what that means?"

"Yeah. I guess."

"So, level with me. Did your parents' breakup make you dumb?"

He gaped at me. "No!"

"Lazy?" I asked.

"I'm not lazy," he snapped.

"Good." I put his borrowed skates back where they went before grabbing my bag. "Because I'm not teaching some dumb, lazy kid hockey. If you want to learn from me, you're gonna have to stay up on your grades, and don't think your bullshit excuses will get you out of anything. Trust me. I was your age once, and I used them all."

He eyed me. "You did? Were you dumb or lazy?"

The shithead turned my own words against me. It was everything I could do to keep from laughing my ass off. Mussing up his hair, I answered, "Neither. I was a smartass little punk who thought I knew all there was to know. Good thing I had a crusty old coach to set me straight."

He grinned up at me. "Good thing I got one of those, too."

12

Tina

I'D BEEN EXPECTING a relaxing spa day with Carisa, but my newfound friend betrayed me. Instead, we drove out to Bellevue, where she parked in front of a massive two-story home and gave me a sheepish smile.

"Where are we?" I asked, looking for some sort of sign that the residence doubled as a spa.

"I'm sorry, Tina. I fucked up."

The hair on the back of my neck rose as the implication of her words hit me. I could only think of one way she could really fuck up: Matt.

No.

That was impossible. She didn't even know about him.

Unless Kaos had said something.

Kaos had delivered the divorce papers to Matt. Had my ex somehow gotten through to him? Maybe they'd exchanged numbers. Matt would no doubt love the opportunity to share his convoluted side of the story. I'd heard him spin a tale and knew perfectly well that he could come out of any situation smelling like roses and innocence. Kaos had been avoiding me all week... disappearing after we dropped Dylan off at school until it was time to pick him up again. Maybe Matt had filled his head with lies, and now Carisa was in on it.

Implausible as the idea was, I couldn't help my brain from fixating on it. After all, I'd never imagined my husband would become some psycho woman beater who was no doubt plotting my murder, but here we were.

"Define effed up," I said. My voice sounded funny. Hollow. My pulse raced and my hands started to tremble.

I didn't think Carisa noticed, because instead of answering my question she climbed out of her car and gestured for me to follow. I didn't. I couldn't. Half expecting Matt to come barging out of the house, I watched the door and willed myself to move. To get the hell out of there.

It felt like I was underwater again, kicking and splashing, about to drown.

My car door opened and Carisa blocked it, concern etched in the lines of her face. "Breathe, Tina."

I filled my lungs with air, shuddering.

"What's wrong?" she asked.

I needed to call Emily. I needed to let her know what was going on.

Surely, she'd help me.

Matt couldn't have possibly gotten to her.

Right?

My phone was peeking out of my purse. I grabbed it, but Carisa waved a hand in front of my face.

"Tina. Snap out of it. What's going on?" She sounded worried. Of course, she'd be worried; she was nice. It wasn't her fault Matt had tricked her. She probably thought she was helping me.

"I know you didn't mean to," I said. "We can still get out of here before he sees me."

"I..." Confusion clouded her expression as she looked from me to the house. "Before *who* sees you?"

"*Him.*" I didn't even want to say his name out loud. I felt like I was Frodo and had just slid the one ring of power onto my finger. Matt's ever-seeing eye was turned my direction, and the instant his name left my lips, I'd summon him.

Carisa was staring at me like I was crazy.

I lowered my voice and whispered, "Matt."

"Matt? Who the hell is Matt?" Her eyes narrowed to slits as the answer seem to come to her. "You mean your... your ex?"

I nodded.

"Tina, why would your ex be at my aunt's house?"

"Your aunt's house?" She sounded legitimately confused. I could relate. "You said you effed up."

"You think I—" Her eyes widened in shock. "No. Fucked up like I accidentally told my cousin, Nora, about you. Not fucked up like I accidentally took you to see your ex!"

"We're at your aunt's house?" I asked again. It felt like I was back in college algebra, being asked to solve for X when the rest of the data was all mixed up.

She glanced at the house. "Yes. Aunt Linore's. She's Darius's mom."

"And Matt's not here?"

"No!" She threw her head back, frustrated. "Look, I told Nora. She told her mom, who told my mom, who told Aunt Linore. They held an impromptu family meeting and decided I had to bring you here to meet everyone. The only people in that house are the nosy, invasive women in my crazy-ass family. I fucked up, because now they're going to be all up in your business, like they are in mine, and I don't want that for you."

Dropping my phone back into my purse, I let out a breath and collapsed against the back of my seat. Now that the threat had been extinguished, I was exhausted. I hated the way my entire body still trembled, but there was no help for that. I'd have to breathe through it until my heart stopped trying to bust out of my chest.

Carisa stared at me like she needed a better explanation for my insane behavior. "The marriage didn't end well," I said, somehow managing to minimize the entirety of my toxic relationship into five little inadequate words.

"I can tell." She scoffed. "What I don't understand is why you think I would sell you out to him. Or to anyone, for that matter."

"I don't. I... It's complicated. Matt is very..." I'd offended her, and I felt bad about that, but I didn't know strong enough words to describe him. To make sense of our bizarre situation. "He always knows what to say. People believe him. I had evidence of his lies, and *I* believed him. He made me question things I saw with my own eyes. He made me feel like I was going crazy. Like I didn't deserve... anything."

Seconds ticked by as I stared at my feet, embarrassed and disgusted with myself. Just talking about him made me feel weak and vulnerable.

Finally, Carisa grabbed me by the shoulders and forced me to meet her gaze. "Darius said your ex was a piece of shit. I get it. The asshole obviously screwed you over good. But you need to understand something. My cousin—who I would walk through fire for—is all about you and your son."

I started to object, but she held up a hand, silencing me. "Don't even try to deny it. I know Darius better than anyone, and I've never seen him like this before. He likes you, and the more I get to know you, the more I understand why. You're good for each other. You have a real shot at happiness. That is a rare thing, and I would never take it away from you. Or him."

My brain tried to process that information, feeding me memories of the way Kaos looked at me. Of the little touches and near misses. Was she right? Was he into me?

It didn't matter. Attraction meant nothing, and there were more pressing matters to deal with. Shelving the possibilities to worry about later, I focused on the problem at hand. "I'm sorry for even assuming... I freaked out, and—" There were so many things I wanted to say, but I lacked the words. A flicker of curtains drew my attention. Apparently, we had an audience. Kaos's family was in there, watching and waiting as I struggled through the effects of my anxiety.

"Don't even worry about it," she said, patting my shoulder. "I know a panic attack when I see one. By the way, you can rest assured that if I ever do meet Matt, I'll cut off his pecker and shove it up his ass for you."

Strangely enough, I didn't doubt her for a minute. Her brassy declaration wiped away the last of my lingering trepidation. I rallied my courage and smiled. "Thank you."

"Oh, it will be my pleasure, trust me. Now, you ready to meet the fam?"

No, I wasn't, not even remotely, but I followed her into the house anyway.

It was a little like stepping into a family-owned restaurant. The atmosphere was warm and inviting, and the air smelled of freshly cooked food, making my stomach rumble. A group of beautiful, olive-skinned women were clustered in the entryway. They opened ranks and enveloped us in a hairspray and perfume haze of introductions.

As soon as I'd met everyone and gave vague, incomplete answers for uncomfortable questions like how long I'd known Darius, and how I'd met him, Carisa passed me a glass of wine. It was before noon, but I had a feeling I'd need it.

Next thing I knew, we were sitting around a massive kitchen table. Soup was served, followed by salad, and then an olive tapenade served with bread and some sort of Greek bruschetta. A foreign fried cheese came next, and then spinach and feta filo. By the time roasted vegetables were added to the table, I was glad I'd worn stretchy pants.

"How many courses will there be?" I asked Carisa, who was seated beside me.

"At least a few more." She smiled. "Might want to take smaller portions and slow down."

Great. "Now you tell me."

She gave me a sheepish smile. "We like to eat."

Next came something called moussaka. It smelled delicious, and I didn't want to offend anyone, but I didn't think I could take another bite.

"This is Aunt Linore's special recipe," Carisa said, adding it to my plate. "It's like an eggplant and beef lasagna."

Linore smiled at me from across the table.

Lowering her voice to a whisper, Carisa added, "You have to at least try it."

Of course, I did. "If I burst, please tell Dylan I love him." I whispered.

"That's a bit dramatic, but okay. Try not to make a mess, though. Exploding in my aunt's home is no way to make brownie points."

"I'll be dead." I pointed out. "I don't think I'll care about making points."

But alive, I did care. Far more than I cared to admit. The ladies around me talked and laughed as they ate, and it was clear to see that they genuinely loved each other. The atmosphere was so comfortable, and everyone seemed relaxed and happy. Despite her previous digs, even Carisa was smiling and chatting it up with her family. My chest ached at the sight. I'd always wanted a big family. Matt was an only child, and his parents lived in the Midwest. They were super reserved and stiff, the kind of people who wouldn't be caught dead gorging themselves at a family get-together like this.

I, on the other hand, loved it.

I devoured the moussaka. Then came fried potatoes, followed by dessert. By the time Carisa dropped me off at Kaos's, my food belly was showing, I was tipsy, my cheeks ached from smiling so much, and I felt warm all over. I found Kaos and Dylan sitting on the sofa in the game room, watching a group of kids play hockey on the television.

"Hey guys," I said, joining them.

"Hi, Mom." Dylan gave me a distracted wave while keeping his attention on the television.

"Hey," Kaos said, looking me up and down. Twice. "You're home later than I expected. How was the spa?"

There was something carnal and forbidden in his gaze, and I wondered if he was aware of the full body goosebumps his twice-over had given me. He had a beer in hand and was back to his low-hanging sweatpants. He'd paired them with a T-shirt that stretched across his pecks in the most delicious way. It took me a moment to realize he'd asked a question, but I finally shook myself and told him where we'd really spent the day.

He groaned, rubbing a hand down his face. "Man. You should have called. I would have put together a rescue party to get you out of there."

"You sound like Carisa. I don't know what's wrong with the two of you, but your family is amazing. No rescue was required."

"Carisa and I lead private lives, and the family doesn't understand things like boundaries and plans that don't include them."

I grinned, seeing where that could be a problem. "Well, I think they're amazing. And I'll probably never need to eat again, so there's that. Your mom sent you leftovers, by the way." I held up the grocery bag full of Tupperware containers she'd sent. "Want me to put these in the fridge?"

"No way!" Kaos jumped out of his seat and headed for the kitchen before I could so much as blink. Moments later, he returned with plates and silverware. Taking the bag from me, he unloaded the goodies. "You hungry, Dylan?" He asked.

Dylan shook his head. He had his elbows on his knees, head in hands, and was glued to the screen. Sitting beside him, I wanted to drill him about how the hockey lessons went, but I'd never seen him so invested in a show. I didn't want to disturb him.

"What are you watching?" I asked Kaos, keeping my voice low as I pointed at the screen.

"*The Mighty Ducks.*"

"The what?" I asked, leaning closer so I was practically behind Dylan.

Kaos looked at me like I'd grown a second head. "You've never seen *The Mighty Ducks* before?" When I shook my head, his face scrunched up in disgust and he finished piling food onto his plate. "I can't believe this. *The Mighty Ducks* is a child's rite of passage. You can't actually grow up until you watch it. Kinda like *The Sandlot*, *The Karate Kid*, and *The Goonies*. Without these experiences, you run the risk of becoming something awful... like a serial killer or a telemarketer."

His goofy explanation paired with a stone-cold serious expression made my eyebrows rise. "Sounds like I have some catching up to do. Is there a list of these rites of passage somewhere?"

"I'll write one up for ya." He took a bite and washed it down with a swallow of beer. I tried really hard not to notice how kissable his lips were or how masculine his Adam's Apple looked bobbing up and down. I'd never found the Adam's Apple particularly attractive before, but everything about Kaos was so hot it short-circuited my brain and made me intensely aware of my body. My mind flickered back to Carisa's declaration that Kaos was into me.

Could it really be true?

I hated the hope that flooded my chest. By now, I should have learned better. I wished there was a button I could push to turn off my emotions and just coast through life for a while without any pain or expectations.

"Thank you," I said lamely.

He gave me a crooked smile. Heat flooded my cheeks as well as my core. I sat back, settling a throw pillow against my stomach like it was a shield that could somehow deflect his charm. Still, it was nice, being there with him and Dylan. Comfortable. We'd been

Centering Kaos

spending evenings together all week, and no matter how hard I tried not to, I looked forward to it.

When Kaos finished eating, he grabbed himself another beer and poured me a glass of wine. It kept my warm and fuzzy buzz going as we watched the Ducks battle it out on the screen against the Hawks. The movie was kind of cheesy, but good.

Dylan loved it. As soon as the credits started rolling on the movie, he jumped up like the couch was on fire and launched into the details of his hockey adventure. While he talked, I shooed him upstairs and toward the bathroom. The dark circles around his eyes told me a hard crash was coming, and I didn't have long to get him bathed and in bed. I started his bath while he undressed. He climbed into the water, and I took in the collection of marks covering his body.

"What happened?" I asked.

"It's only a couple of bruises," he said. "You should have seen me. I only fell a couple of times. Kaos says I'm a natural."

Not what I wanted to hear. If skating without sticks and opponents had given him that many bruises, I didn't even want to see what he'd look like after an actual hockey practice. Leaning against the door, I tried to keep my expression neutral despite my concern. My life would be much easier if Dylan had hated the entire experience, but that was clearly not the case. He was like an excited little jumping bean, barely able to sit still as he carried on about his plans to become the biggest star the NHL had ever seen.

I just wanted to wrap him in Styrofoam and bubble wrap.

Hockey seemed so dangerous.

And expensive.

I'd done a little research, and I didn't know what the going rate for souls was these days, but I'd need to sell mine to come up with a down payment for the gear alone. Not to mention ice time and coaching. According to the internet, hockey was the second most expensive sport a kid could play. Not reassuring when my bank account was barely in the black. Kaos had volunteered to coach Dylan for free—which would eliminate some of the cost—but the man was already letting us stay in his house and eat his food. This felt a lot like taking advantage of his kindness and generosity.

I needed to figure out a way to stand on my own two feet.

Worry churned my stomach. The car insurance payment was coming due, and I had no idea how to pay it. Especially since I no longer had a job. I'd called Mr. Denali earlier in the week and quit. Probably not the smartest decision I'd ever made, but Matt's latest attack had brought on a string of nightmares I couldn't shake. I wanted to work—needed to work—but I also needed to live. A paycheck wouldn't do much for me if Matt caught me in the parking garage again and finished what he'd started.

Health insurance was also a problem. Hockey most likely meant broken bones, concussions, and stitches. We currently had coverage through Matt's work, but he could remove us in a blink, and I wouldn't even know. At least, not until I showed up in the emergency room with Dylan's bone poking through his leg only to find out our coverage was denied.

Dylan was staring at me expectantly. Right. While I'd been on the verge of a nervous breakdown, he'd been carrying on about all the fun he'd had.

"I'm glad you enjoyed skating," I lied. I'd seen a broken bone poking through the skin once. That wasn't something you forgot. I would freak out if something like that ever happened to my child.

Dylan settled down, his previous joy leaking out of his expression. "You don't seem glad."

It had been far too long since I'd seen him so excited, and I felt like the worst mom ever for letting my reality get in the way of his happiness. Silently vowing to do better, I forced a smile. "Sorry, bud. I'm just tired. It's been a long day. Come on. Let's get you out of there." I held up a towel for him to step into.

"I like living with Kaos," Dylan announced. "I think we should stay here forever."

Shocked, I stared at him. He hadn't asked about his dad all week, but I never would have imagined he'd want to stay with Kaos.

"He's nice, Mom. His house is safe." Dylan met my gaze, his big green eyes solemn and honest. "You don't even fall down the stairs here."

My chest squeezed, sucking all the oxygen out of my lungs. The first time Matt had beaten me, he'd fed that lie to our son. I'd never corrected him... never told Dylan that it wasn't the stairs.

But I always wondered if he knew the truth.

Dylan wasn't stupid, after all, and after Matt had tried to kidnap him from the park...

Dylan yawned and headed into his bedroom. Still in a daze, I followed. He dressed in pajamas and handed me his wet towel. On autopilot, I took it to the bathroom and hung it up before returning to tuck my son in. I kissed his forehead and headed for the door.

Someone knocked.

Dylan cried out, "Come in!" as I braced myself.

"Hey, buddy, you wanted me to come in and tell you goodnight?" he said, still holding onto the door.

"Yeah." Dylan nodded, gesturing for Kaos to come closer. As Kaos approached, my son said, "I've been thinking about it, and I want a hockey name, too."

"You do, huh?" Kaos asked with a barely suppressed smile.

He met my gaze and my knees felt weak.

You don't even fall down the stairs here, Dylan's voice said in the back of my mind. It played on a loop, reminding me that my son was observant. He saw way more than he should, and had to be picking up on the emotions between me and Kaos.

"You got a name in mind?" Kaos asked.

"Mayhem," Dylan replied.

Kaos chuckled. "That's one you're gonna have to earn, buddy. We'll talk about it the next time we get you on the ice. You thought anymore about those turns I showed you?"

He was so good with Dylan it made my heart ache. Was this

what a dad was supposed to be like? I'd never had one and I didn't know...

But Kaos wasn't Dylan's dad. He was just a good man, letting us stay in his house. There might be feelings developing between us, but it was too soon for all that. Hadn't I learned my lesson the last time?

I needed to get out of there... to go somewhere I could get my head on straight and my emotions under control. They were talking about stretches when I slipped out.

13

Kaos

MAN CAVES ARE traditionally located in basements or garages. Mine could be found on the third-floor landing of my house. Dark wooden shelves stocked with pictures, awards, and memorabilia from my hockey and Army days lined one full wall of the room, reminding me of where I'd been and what I'd accomplished. The opposite wall held a seventy-seven inch, 4k television, adjacent to a built-in fully stocked bar. It had been a major selling point of the house. Not because I was a lush or anything, but because it looked classy and grown up, and twenty-four-year-old me had been desperate to be seen as an adult.

Slipping behind the bar, I eyed the beer fridge, immediately dismissing it. The three beers I'd already drunk had done nothing for me. Tonight called for something stronger.

I wasn't usually much of a drinker. Sure, I enjoyed the taste of a fine scotch or bourbon as much as the next guy, but I rarely overindulged. The last time I'd been rip-roaring drunk had come with four years of consequences, teaching me to pay closer attention to my limits. A wiser man would have marched right past the bar and locked himself in his bedroom, but unfortunately, I lacked both wisdom and willpower at the moment. I went straight for the hard shit, pouring myself a tumbler of twenty-five-year-old single-malt scotch. Flavor exploded on my tongue before burning all the way down.

It was some good shit.

Skating with Dylan had left me feeling sticky and in need of a shower. Leaving my glass on the bar, I headed through my attached bedroom and into the bathroom, shedding clothes as I went. Jerking off in the shower had become a necessity since Tina moved in, and as I stepped beneath the stream, my cock immediately rose to the occasion. With my thoughts affixed on her curves, it only took a couple of minutes to rub one out. The release helped sate my need, but it was far from satisfying. Kind of like settling for a salad when your body's craving steak and potatoes that'll stick to your ribs and last a while. Sure, the snack would keep me from starving to death, but it wasn't what I wanted—what I needed—and I'd be hungry again in no time.

Toweling off, I slipped on a pair of sweats and headed back into my man cave. I wanted to keep walking... head right down those stairs and knock on Tina's bedroom door. The more I thought about it, the harder it was to remember why that'd be a bad idea. Forcing myself to sit my ass down on a barstool, I considered my options and changed objectives.

Tonight, drinking wasn't about enjoying a glass of good scotch.

No. If I was going to drink, I needed to get my ass so drunk I couldn't move. That way, I'd have no choice but to stay upstairs and away from her. Plan in place, I let the liquor burn away my thoughts as I pulled out my phone and selected a playlist, connecting it to the surround sound. The feel-good vibes of Hawaiian music filtered through the room, easing some of the tension from my shoulders. I relaxed, letting the tunes carry away my worries while I drank alone.

Only I wasn't alone for long.

As I finished the last of my second glass, Tina called out my name, her voice sounding uncertain as it rose up the stairwell from below. Turning, I spotted the top of her head. As she climbed, the rest of her appeared in a tantalizing reveal that had my full attention. She'd changed into a pair of sleep shorts that showed off her shapely legs and a loose T-shirt that did little to hide the fact she wasn't wearing a bra. Especially with her still wet hair dripping on it.

My dick instantly hardened at the sight. She wasn't a fucking salad; she was the steak and potatoes my body kept craving. And I was so damn starving I had no hopes of resisting her.

Thankfully, I didn't appear to be the only one suffering.

I'd neglected to put on a shirt after my shower, and she was staring at my chest like she wanted to lick it.

Good. Let her be in agony alongside me.

Besides, even if I wanted to end her misery, standing was out of the question. I wasn't wearing underwear, and the minute I stood, the tent in my sweatpants would be obvious as fuck. I kept my ass on the stool like a rude motherfucker, just trying to will away my boner.

She halted, taking in the space. I had no idea why she was there. She'd never come up to my lair before, and I sure as hell hadn't been expecting a visit tonight. It couldn't be Dylan. He fell asleep mid-sentence before I left his room. Judging by how exhausted the kid was, he was down for the count.

"Is everything okay?" I asked, hoping Matt hadn't found a way to contact her.

Dragging her gaze up to meet mine, she nodded uncertainly. "Oh. Yeah. Everything's fine. Great, even. I just... I came up here because I wanted to thank you."

I tried to focus on the pink of her cheeks, rather than the pebbling of her nipples beneath her thin shirt, but it was a struggle. "To thank me?"

"Yep." Another nod, this one more vigorous. "For helping Dylan today. Taking the time to work with him on the ice... it means the world to him. And to... to me. I know you said there's no charge for coaching him, but I will pay you. Once I get back on my feet, I mean."

God, her lips were fucking perfect. Every word they formed made me want to taste them. To see how they'd look against my skin. To watch them sliding up and down my cock. If she wanted to pay me, I could think of a few ways she could do it.

And fuck, I couldn't believe my mind had gone there. But I couldn't help it, either. I was so fucking desperate to touch her, I would have lied, stolen, or murdered for the chance. Extortion seemed like a drop in the bucket, comparatively.

"You never have to thank me for that. I enjoy hanging out with the kid." I needed to shoo her ass back downstairs, but I didn't have that kind of strength or self-preservation. Instead, I gestured at my glass. "Can I buy you a drink?"

I expected her to refuse—hoped and feared she would—but she didn't. Instead, she perked up. "Do you have wine up here? That's what I've been drinking, so I should probably stick with it."

A little voice in the back of my mind kept pointing out that drinking with Tina was a very bad idea. Having never cared much for restrictions and limitations, I shut that little bastard down and nodded. "I've got just the thing." Spinning my barstool to face away from her before standing, I tried to be discreet and not give her a show as I slipped behind the bar and poured her a glass of my favorite red blend.

When I turned back around, Tina had settled onto a barstool, looking like she planned to be there awhile. Accepting the glass, she sipped and beamed a smile at me.

A real smile.

It was the first one she'd ever blessed me with, and it stole my goddamn breath away.

Tina was gorgeous on a bad day, but that smile... holy shit, the woman was fucking radiant. I had to fight the urge to take a page from *Wayne's World* and bow at her feet, chanting, 'I'm not worthy.' Instead, I calmly got myself together, refreshed my drink, and sat beside her. The clean, fresh scent of her soap wrapped around me, teasing and threatening to bring me to my knees.

"This is really good," she said, angling her wine glass toward me. "Thank you."

I nodded. "You're welcome. It's my favorite. I hide it up here so Carisa can't find it."

"She doesn't clean up here?" Tina asked.

"Oh, she does, and I'm sure she knows about the wine, but she... she respects the power of the man cave."

"Ah." Tina's eyes lit up with laughter as she looked around again. "I hope my presence here isn't somehow disrespectful to the power of the man cave."

"Not at all," I admitted. "Strong, beautiful women only enhance the power of the man cave."

She frowned at her glass. Not exactly the reaction I was going for.

I nudged her with my shoulder. "What's that look for?"

She shrugged. "Nothing."

"Come on. I'm the bartender tonight, which means you can tell me anything. Falls under bartender – patron confidentiality."

A smile tugged at the corner of her lips. "It does, huh?"

"Absolutely. Bartenders have big ears and short memories. Whatever you say in this space, stays here. It's the law. So, tell me what that look was for."

She took another sip. "Well, I don't feel very strong or beautiful." She winced. "But that sounds like I'm fishing for compliments, and I'm not trying to do that. I'm just... I'm just a mess."

"Aren't we all?"

Her head whipped around, and she met my gaze. "You're not."

"You don't think so?"

"No." She gestured toward my wall of memorabilia. "You've won medals, earned your bachelor's degree, served our country, and you have the resources and ability to help others. You've lived on your terms, and you didn't let anyone hold you back."

"Yeah, but I've also never had anyone to share my accomplishments with," I admitted. "Living life on your own terms can get really fuckin' lonely at times."

I probably shouldn't have said it—shouldn't have opened up and shown her that vulnerability—but being around her and Dylan had really highlighted all the shit I'd missed out on. Besides, there was no taking my words back now. We sat in silence for a while, nursing our drinks as Tina bobbed her head to the music.

"You like this song?" I asked.

"Never heard it before, but it's catchy. Surprising, though."

"Why surprising?" I asked.

"It's mellow and... upbeat. Aren't bikers supposed to be into something a little darker and more anti-establishment? Shouldn't you be up here raging against the machine or planning out your route on the highway to hell?"

I chuckled. "You sure do have some interesting theories about bikers."

She winced. "Sorry. I didn't mean for that to come out as judgy. I was really just messing with you. The bikers from your club seem... nice."

She'd only met me, Tap, and Rabbit. Tap could probably be defined as nice, but Rabbit... Rabbit was fucking crazy. "No, you're right. Rock and metal are usually what they play at the fire station, but I was a hockey player long before I was a biker. Had a teammate who introduced me to these tunes. Now, it's what I listen to when I need to chill the fuck out."

Her brow furrowed as she sipped wine. "Are you stressed about something?"

Not so much stressed as horny. And frustrated. "Just got a lot on my mind."

"We're not..." She seemed to struggle with the words. "If our being here is stressing you out—"

Centering Kaos

"It's not," I said, putting an end to that line of her thinking. "I like having you guys here. Breaks up the monotony and gives me someone to talk to. It's nice."

That seemed to appease her. She turned away, studying my wall of memorabilia. After a time, she asked, "What made you join the Army?"

It was one hell of an abrupt change of subject, and I cocked my head to the side, wondering what she wanted to hear.

"I mean, you clearly didn't need the service to pay for your college. Were you after a certain experience? Or are you one of those wannabe superhero types?" The smile playing on her lips softened her words. I couldn't tell if she was flirting with me or what.

"No. It's nuthin' as honorable as a superhero complex." In fact, it was downright embarrassing, but I refused to sugar coat it or lie to her. "You sure you want to know? You're probably gonna be disappointed. Might not ever look at me the same way again."

"Oh?" She quirked an eyebrow at me. "Now I'm definitely interested. Do tell."

"Well, I had a bit of an ego back before I joined the Army."

She leaned closer, giving me a close up of her bright, hazel eyes, and it took everything in me not to fucking drown in them. "I'd imagine an ego is a requirement for athletes who play professional sports," she said.

I smiled. "Thanks, but there's no need to make excuses for my shitty behavior. Too many people let it slide over the years, and their leni... lenien..." Unable to get my tongue to form the word, I gave up. "And that shit didn't do me any favors. Nowadays, I try to surround myself with people honest enough to knock me down a peg or two whenever I get to thinkin' I'm all high and mighty."

"Carisa..."

"She doesn't knock me down a peg or two. She shoves me down the whole fuckin' ladder, then beats me with it for my trouble." My smile turned into a chuckle as I shook my head. "But yeah, I appreciate the hell out of her for it. Anyway, the team I was with decided not to renew my contract. My agent had secured a couple of other offers, but they were nowhere near what I thought I was worth. I was at the bar, throwin' a fuckin' toddler-sized tantrum and feeding my anger with whiskey when an Army recruiter plopped himself down on the stool next to me. He introduced himself, and some sort of dumbass bullshit came out of my mouth, sounding a lot like, 'Oh, I always wanted to join the Army'."

Tina giggled. Fucking giggled. It was the sweetest, most authentic, most musical sound I'd ever heard. I froze, staring at her and gobbling up every blessed second of it. She noticed, and her cheeks turned bright red. Straightening, she cleared her throat and said, "Continue."

I needed to find a way to make her giggle again.

"Well, the recruiter pointed out that I wasn't too old to join. My whiskey-to-brain-cell ratio was way out of whack, and I was pissed at the entire world for not recognizing me for the next Wayne Gretzky that I thought I was." Okay, so that was a bit of an exaggeration, but her covered smiles and coughing laughter made it well worth it. I couldn't tell if she was tipsy, or if I was so drunk I'd become a comedian, but it was working, so I ran with it. "Gave him my name, number, and email address, promising to come to his office the next day to sign up."

Tina's eyes widened hysterically. "You didn't. I heard those guys are ruthless!"

"I did." I finished off my scotch and stood to refill our glasses. The room swayed a little, but I got my bearings. "And he didn't even get the chance to be ruthless because I made the mistake of calling my dad and telling him I was enlisting." She cocked her head, expression confused, as if not understanding how my dad came into play, so I explained. "You gotta understand, my dad isn't big on hockey. He was proud of the money and success I earned, but he saw sports as a child's pastime. He wanted more for me. A man's job."

"That's so weird," she said. "I don't understand why people are like that. You weren't starving, you were getting paid big bucks for doing what you love, and you were happy. Why not be happy for you? No matter what Dylan does, I'm gonna be proud of him."

"Thank you," I said, feeling vindicated. "But unfortunately, most parents have more... requirements for their children than happiness. Dad was so goddamn proud of me for enlisting. Prouder than I'd ever heard him be. He had that tone... the one he gets whenever one of my brothers does something to make him proud. I'd been workin' my whole life to hear that tone directed at me, and I..." I shook my head. "I couldn't let him down."

She stared at me like I was speaking in another language. "You joined the Army to make your dad proud?"

"Sure did. It's not as rare as you'd think. People do all kinds of crazy shit to make their parents happy."

"But you could have died."

I neglected to mention that I almost did. "Coulda died driving to the school or practice. Coulda died crossing the road to get the mail."

"Pretty sure the odds are much higher when you're on active duty."

She had a point, so I shrugged.

Tina sat back, frowning, and I could almost see the wheels spinning in her head.

"What's wrong?" I asked.

"Do you think Dylan's always gonna want to make his dad proud?"

Just thinking about that piece of shit having any control whatsoever of Dylan's emotional security made me grind my teeth. Matt didn't deserve a kid as cool as Dylan.

Or a wife as sweet and caring as Tina.

Instead of answering her question, I blurted out one of my own. "Why'd you marry him?"

Her eyebrows rose.

"I mean... forget that. Fuck. You don't have to tell me nuthin'. Excuse my nosy ass and pretend I didn't ask."

"No." She drained the last of her wine. "I want to explain. He... You have to understand... he wasn't that bad."

"Okay." Talk about the last thing I wanted to hear from her mouth. Not that bad? The fucker had tried to strangle her.

"At least, not at first," she corrected. "I... I met him at a party my sophomore year of college. I hadn't been to many parties, and I was young, inexperienced, and it was all so overwhelming. Er... that's what I thought. Turned out the room was spinning from more than cheap booze and social anxiety. Someone roofied me. I don't remember much about the experience."

"Shit."

"Yeah, but I got lucky." She grabbed my arm, and her hands felt good around my bicep. Comfortable, like they were meant to be there. "Matt found me passed out in a corner, and he took me to his apartment. Put me in his bed and let me sleep it off."

"I'll bet he did."

"He didn't try anything." She gave my arm a squeeze. "When I woke up, I was fully dressed and... nothing had happened. He didn't take advantage of my situation. He brought me Gatorade and soup and let me hang out there until I recovered. Then, he asked me out. I wasn't really into him, but he was nice, and he'd rescued me from what could have been a very bad situation. I felt like I owed him a shot."

"Like hell!" I stood to refill our drinks. "If I ever have a daughter, the first thing I'm gonna teach her is that she doesn't owe anyone shit. I don't know why society teaches girls to be grateful when boys act like decent human beings. Helping someone who's drugged is basic human decency. It shouldn't qualify him for some claim on your life." I was getting worked up, but the whole scenario sounded a little too convenient to me. "You sure he's not the one who roofied you in the first place? Maybe he wanted to show up and play hero."

I'd been around the block enough times to know how common that was.

She shrugged. "I've thought about it, but there's no way to know for sure. He shouldn't have even been at that party. He wasn't a student. He'd already gotten his degree and was working for a big tech company. Strangely enough, he looked familiar. I could have sworn I'd seen him around campus." She shook her head. "Anyway, he was really nice. He opened doors, paid for dinners, and made me feel like I was something special. I'd been so focused on my education, but... he was an unexpected distraction. There was no spark or magic or anything, but I didn't really believe in all of that. I thought we could build something."

A spark didn't even begin to describe what I felt for Tina. And I had a pretty good idea she felt the same. She said she didn't believe in it—past tense—but I wondered if she was a believer now. The question lingered on the tip of my tongue, but I refused to ask it. She was finally letting me in, and I didn't want her to clam up again.

"Then one thing led to another, and I got pregnant. He was really happy about the baby, and he convinced me to drop out of school and move in with him. He came from money and had a great job. He wanted to support us."

It was difficult to reconcile the asshole who'd beat her with this storybook version of him. "He sounds great." That came out sounding a little more sarcastic than I'd meant for it to, but I was ready for the rest of the story. The part where she focused on his sins and vowed to never go back to his abusive ass.

"No. He was never great. Something about him was always... off. There were plenty of red flags, but I lowered my head and ran right through those suckers. Supporting turned into controlling really fast, but I stuck my head in the ground like an ostrich and let it happen. Growing up without a strong family unit made me really want one, you know? I wanted to be a good wife and a mom and

Matt had this way of making me feel like I needed to try harder. To do what he said and keep the peace."

I snorted. "Pretty sure that's called gaslighting."

She nodded. "I don't even know how I let it get that far. But one day, I popped my head out of the ground to realize that in my desire to make Matt happy, I'd totally lost myself. I'd given up my education, I was stuck in the house without transportation or friends, and nothing I said or did seemed to make him happy. I don't even understand why he wants me back. In the past five years, we've barely even talked. I made his meals and cleaned his house, but he could hire someone for that."

Not someone he could beat. Not unless your prostitute look-alike can cook and clean.

Her brow furrowed, and she shook herself. "I'm sorry."

"For what?" I asked.

Blowing out a breath, she looked away. "I dunno. Losing myself. Failing at marriage. Putting up with so much. Not enduring through more. Boring you with my pathetic life story. Everything. I'm sorry for it all."

I stared at her, wondering what to say to take some of the weight from her shoulders. She looked like the god Atlas, carrying the whole damn world on her back. I didn't think it was wise for her to spend too much time poring over her past. She couldn't change it. All she could do was beat herself up over it, and I had a feeling she'd done that enough.

Thankfully, as I was searching my alcohol-muddled brain for some pearl of wisdom to share, one of my favorite songs came on, giving me an idea. It was time to get off this fucked-up topic. We couldn't do shit about her past, but we could make her present a little more enjoyable. Since all the talk about her ex had taken down the tent in my pants, I stood. Offering her my hand, I asked, "Dance with me?"

Confusion registered across her face before excitement lit up her eyes. "You want to dance?"

I nodded, emboldened by the smile that tugged at her lips. "It's been a minute, and I don't know if I'm any good at it anymore, but yeah. Why the fuck not?"

Sliding off the stool, she put her hand in mine. It looked so pale and small, and I marveled at the courage it must have taken her to even come up these stairs. Matt had screwed her over good, but she was still so damn trusting. I led her to the middle of the floor, restarted the song, and turned up the volume. Then, as we swayed with the music, I met her gaze and started singing along with the lyrics.

"Girl don't you worry. The world is a dangerous place, but I'm gonna keep you safe," I sang.

She brushed against the front of me and I realized dancing probably wasn't the smartest idea. Having her this close was starting to stir up activity down below again.

I tried to focus on the song, but the sweetest smile tugged at her lips. "What is this?"

"Common Kings. *Happy Pill*. Now shush. You're ruining it." I restarted the song again.

Tina snickered, and then full-on laughed out loud when I twirled her around before pulling her back to me.

God, the feel of her in my arms was torture. The sound of her laughter was much better than the self-doubt and pain I'd heard in her voice during story time. I liked making her laugh. But as I kept singing, offering to be the happy pill she took whenever she felt like she was about to break, tears filled her eyes. She blinked them away, but not before one fell. Needing more of her smiles and less of her tears, I went a little over-the-top, acting out parts of the song as I sang.

"These are some fucked up times." Trying to keep her body away from growing erection, I spun her over to the bar and picked up the empty wine bottle and pretended to pour more into her glass. "So let me pour you some red wine."

She laughed as I put down the bottle and whirled us back out to the center of the room. Two spins in a row had been a little ambitious for our combined blood alcohol levels, and I almost put us both on the floor. Bumping against the wall, I was careful to shield Tina, but popped off with a string of swear words as I stubbed my toe.

Her laughter only increased. Tears freely ran down her cheeks, but they were happy tears now. I stopped to watch her, marveling at how she could still laugh. After everything she'd been through, she could still let it all go and just... laugh.

With the pad of my thumb, I wiped the moisture from her cheek.

Her breath caught. Laughter dying on her parted lips, she stared up at me. The song played out and the next one began as the air thickened with tension and I became fully aware of all the places our bodies touched, and the very few articles of clothing that separated us.

I could feel her nipples harden through her thin T-shirt.

My erection had returned with a vengeance, and my sweats did little to hide it. I could smell her arousal through her sleep shorts. The rest of the world seemed to stand still as Tina's gaze dropped to my lips. Her eyes dilated. Heat poured off her body. We both leaned in, slow and cautious, as if afraid of moving too quickly and destroying the moment.

Then her soft lips met mine, and all bets were off.

Need spiked through my body. The scotch and wine-laced kiss went from sweet and delicate to wild and ravenous. Wet. All-consuming. Her hands landed on my chest and started roaming—searching—scorching. Mine went down her back to the globes of her ass. Tugging upward, I picked her up. She wrapped her legs around my waist as our tongues continued their frantic dance. With the heat of her core grinding against me, it was all I could do to make it through the doorway to my bedroom.

Lowering her to stand in front of the bed, we came apart long enough for me to rip off her shirt. I only got to marvel at her perfect breasts for a moment before our mouths mashed together again. My hands found her tits, feeling the weight, kneading the flesh, plucking at her sexy pink nipples. She groaned and writhed against me, her fingers sliding beneath the waistband of my sweats.

I grabbed her arms, pinning them to her sides. We'd both had a lot to drink, and I needed to make sure she wouldn't regret this. Even though it was torture to move away from her, I pulled back far enough to search her face. "Are you sure this is okay?" I asked.

She nodded, and started inching my sweats down.

I stopped her again. "I need to hear you, to know you really want this. That you... you want me."

"I do." The lust in her eyes was killing me, making my dick so hard it throbbed. "I want this... want you, Darius."

For the first time ever, she'd called me by my real name; that had to mean she knew what she was doing. Still, I wanted a hell of a lot more than one night with her, so I had to make absolute certain. "You sure that's not the alcohol talking?"

"Yes. No, I mean. It's me. I... I want you."

I chuckled, shaking my head. "Not good enough. What about me do you want?"

Her expression tortured, she stared up at me. "You know what I want."

"I do. More than that, I know what you need. But *I* need to hear the words, angel."

"Fine." She shoved my sweats down, leaving me in my birthday suit. My cock sprang up, ready and willing. Her eyes widened at the sight and her hands reached for it, but I kept my grip on her arms and held myself just out of reach.

"The words."

Her breath came out in a frustrated huff before she finally caved. "I fucking want you to fuck me, okay?" she shouted, sounding slightly on the feral side.

It was the first time I'd ever heard her drop the f-bomb, and it was sexy as hell. In answer, I shoved her shorts down. There. Now we were both naked. I picked her ass up and tossed her on the bed. I wanted to take my time and worship every inch of her body, but my body had other plans. I needed to be inside her. Now. I needed to claim her, to make her mine in the most animalistic sense of the word.

My cock leaked as I reached for my nightstand drawer.

"What are you doing?" Tina asked.

"Condom," I replied.

"Latex allergy. I have an IUD and I'm clean."

Fuck me. I'd get to ride her bareback? This kept getting better and better. "Me too."

She nodded, meeting my gaze. "I trust you."

Something inside me snapped, some final wall I'd been keeping between us. Earning her trust made me feel like a king. She was my throne, my crown, the very life blood of my kingdom. I would wage war to prove my fealty. But first, I had to claim her. I lined myself up at her entrance and slowly sank into her wet heat.

She felt so good—so damn good—that it was all I could do to go slow. I didn't want to hurt her, but a part of me wanted to pound her pussy until she had no doubt about where she belonged. About who she belonged to.

I wanted to write my name all over her in permanent ink. Also in cum. She made me feel so fucking feral. Savage.

"More," she whispered. "Harder."

Magic words. I let them drive me as we chased our releases. Kissing, grinding, grunting. She moaned and dug her fingers into my back. I plunged into her harder. Faster. Driving us both insane until the bottom of my spine tingled, and darkness clouded the edges of my vision. I wouldn't last much longer. I couldn't. Not with the sounds she kept making and the way she felt wrapped around my cock.

"Get there for me, angel," I said. "Come for me."

She did, tightening around my cock until I saw stars. I emptied myself inside her with a shout, resting on my arms. I wanted to stay connected to her but didn't want to squash her beneath my weight, so I rolled us until I was on my back with her lying on top of me.

With her head resting against my chest, she muttered something.

"What was that?" I asked.

"Beer before liquor, never been sicker," she repeated. "You're gonna be feelin' that scotch in the morning."

I hadn't exactly been expecting any declarations of undying love, but her words did leave me a little disappointed. "Worth it." I kissed her forehead.

"Very worth it," she agreed, making me feel better.

I'd take it. For now.

I was still smiling when I drifted off to sleep.

14

Tina

LIGHT FILTERED IN through my closed eyelids, blinding me. Despite the incessant throbbing of my brain against my skull, I woke up feeling warm and cozy, more comfortable and satisfied than I'd been in recent memory. Something tickled my nose. Opening my eyes, I saw a spattering of short, curly dark hair. My hand rested against warm flesh over hard muscle.

There was a body beneath me.

Not Matt.

That much was clear. Even as my brain made the deduction, panic still surged through my system, engaging my senses and preparing my reflexes for fight or flight. I held perfectly still, petrified and taking in my surroundings. The room was foreign. I'd never been in it, but I recognized the black and grey color scheme that was consistent throughout the rest of the house.

Kaos's room.

I was in his bed.

I breathed in, and the heady, masculine scent of him sent a wave of want crashing through me even as the ache between my legs and the lingering scent of sex made it clear we'd already done the deed.

Snippets from last night came flooding back to me. Kaos pouring me a glass of wine. Laughter. Dancing. Longing. His eyes—so dark, consuming, and full of emotion—staring down at me.

"Are you sure this is okay?" he asked.

He kept trying to pull away... to do the right thing.

My body thrummed with need as I grabbed ahold of him and told him the truth.

"I fucking want you to fuck me!"

Well then. My cheeks ignited, threatening to burn right off my face. I'd been so forward and... demanding. What the heck? Where had that come from?

The wine.

There must have been some kind of demon in that vino. It possessed me and turned me into some sort of sex-crazed maniac with a filthy mouth. That was the only explanation.

What have I done?

Regret. Fear. Pain. Excitement. It all came crashing into me at once. I felt dirty, but also a little... freed. A voice in the back of my mind kept whispering that I'd loved every forbidden second of it. Heat pooled between my legs in confirmation as I focused on how I'd felt having his undivided attention on me.

His stare had been so intense. And the way he looked into my eyes when he sang to me... the way he filled me up so completely when he...

Oh. My. God!

Yep. I'd loved every second. Every caress, every whisper, every kiss.

Only I couldn't love it.

I wasn't even divorced yet. And Dylan...

Gah!

Careful not to wake Kaos, I scrambled off the bed as quickly as possible. Each shift of my body reminded me of the wonderful soreness between my legs.

Not wonderful, bad. Very bad.

I'm a whore.

A disgusting, horrible whore.

My gaze snagged on Kaos. Lying there in all his naked glory, his body on full display for my viewing pleasure, he looked like some kind of Greek god. The kind women were helpless to resist. My attention went straight to his cock, which was currently sporting some serious morning wood. Had he been like that when I rolled off him? Holy crap! How did he not impale me on that thing? It was enormous—really—at least twice the size of Matt's.

Maybe that was why Matt was always so angry. The little dick energy was real with that one.

A giggle bubbled up my throat.

Was I still drunk?

I gave Kaos's perfect body one last lingering look, wishing things were different. Wishing I'd never met Matt. Only without Matt, there'd be no Dylan, and I didn't even want to consider a reality without my boy.

Holy crap this was a mess. My life was a forest fire, and no matter how I tried to control it, I kept adding fuel to the flames. Last night, I was out of my mind when I'd climbed those stairs. Lonely, weary, and drunk, I'd dropped my guard and let myself feel... hopeful. For what, I still didn't know. But Kaos had been shirtless, and the sight of his bare chest would tempt even the purest of nuns. And based on the way my gaze kept drifting south of his waist, I was no nun.

And that song he sang to me...

All that talk about pulling me close and keeping me safe had been too much. Nobody had offered to shield me before, and although I knew it was just some silly song, his intentions had felt so... real. My thoughts were a mess, condemning, and then excusing my behavior in circles. I needed to get out of there so I could properly evaluate the situation and determine what to do.

Clothes.

I needed my clothes. I started searching the room for them, and my knee popped. Loudly.

Kaos stirred.

I dropped to the floor, out of his line of sight, and held my breath. The instantaneous change in elevation sent invisible spikes through my pounding head, but I held my breath and squeezed my eyes closed against the pain. It ebbed, but still I waited, listening and praying Kaos wouldn't wake up.

I wasn't ready to face him yet.

Truth be told, I didn't know if I'd ever be ready to face him again.

Therein lies the problem. How could I live with someone I couldn't face?

I'd need to move, to find somewhere else to stay.

The thought of leaving him sent a searing hot arrow right through my chest. How on earth had I let him get so close? Even before we... um... took our relationship horizontal, I'd felt something for him. Now, that something felt out of control. Maybe if I put some space between us, I could get my emotions under control again. My gaze locked on the bed, I waited. No movement, no sound. Grateful to be in the clear, I naked army-crawled toward a piece of fabric that I suspected of being my shirt.

Naked. Army-crawled. Across the bedroom floor of a man I'd known for a week. While my son slept downstairs. That was the position my life choices had put me in.

I'm so going to hell for this.

Reaching the fabric, I snatched it up and started to put it over my head. The front fell open like a vest, because it had been ripped apart. Okay, I vaguely remembered that, too.

What were we? Animals?

It wasn't like I had an abundance of clothing that he could just rip apart. But now that I thought about it, the memory of him literally ripping off my shirt sent little flickers of fire straight to my nether regions. Yes, apparently, I was an animal. In heat, even. Trying desperately to ignore my body's reaction, I spied my shorts across the room and set out at a slow, quiet pace to retrieve them. I'd almost made it when the bed shifted.

I rolled, angling toward the space beneath the bed, but Kaos's head popped down right in front of me, blocking my path and ripping a surprised scream from my throat.

Eyes wide, expression confused, he stared at me. "Um, what... What's goin' on, angel?" he asked.

Since I couldn't very well say *I'm army crawling naked across your floor*, I replied with a super intelligent sounding, "What do you mean?"

The side of his lips quirked. "You... you're naked. And lying on my floor. Is something wrong with my bed?"

It was a perfectly reasonable question, but answering it would require admitting I'd previously been in his bed. I was kind of hoping he was too drunk to remember last night's activities. "Aren't you hungover?" I asked.

He cocked his head to the side and studied me like I was a complicated puzzle. "It was good booze and I'm a big guy. I've got a bit of a headache, but it's not too bad. You?"

"I uh... same."

"Want me to get you some ibuprofen?"

I was trying to sneak out of his bedroom after sex, and he was still being sweet and trying to take care of me. Maybe I could use that to my benefit. "No. Thank you. But if you would please turn around for a minute, so I could get up..."

His eyebrows rose. "You want me to turn around?"

If my face got any hotter, it would combust. "Yes. Please."

"You realize I've seen and touched every inch of your beautiful body, right?"

Did he have to be so blunt? "Yes, but that was last night."

"And...?"

"It was dark. It's daytime now. I'm shy."

His eyes narrowed, and I got the feeling he hadn't fallen for my explanation, but he turned anyway. I bolted for my shorts. Scooping them up, I jumped to my feet, but my head rebelled. Leaning against the wall, I took a few measured breaths, trying to keep from throwing up all over his floor. Finally, the room stopped spinning long enough for me to slide my shorts up and hold my shirt closed.

"Can I turn back around yet?" Kaos asked when I stopped moving.

I nodded, realized he couldn't see me, and answered, "Yes."

When his gaze landed on me, I caught a hint of disappointment in his eyes. "You're leaving." It wasn't a question, and he sounded resigned. Good. He must have come to the same conclusion I had.

"Yes. It'll only take me a few minutes to get our stuff together, but I... I think that's for the best."

His eyes widened and he shoved himself up to his knees, giving me a world class view of the most impressive body I'd ever laid eyes on. He was hard—everywhere—and it was almost impossible to look away. "What are you talking about?" he asked.

I didn't understand his sudden confusion. "Dylan and I are leaving... going back to Elenore's."

"Like hell you are," he replied.

Shocked, I stared at him. The part of me that hated confrontation and wanted everyone to be happy and live in peace kept trying to point out that Dylan and I should stay. After all, Kaos had done a lot for us, and we owed him. What had he said about that last night? Oh yeah.

"I don't know why society teaches girls to be grateful when boys act like decent human beings."

I couldn't stay because I felt indebted to him. I'd gone down that road before and knew it ended in a big, fat dead end. I wouldn't let another man control my life. Not ever. Not even someone as good and incredible as Kaos. Squaring my shoulders, I summoned every ounce of resolve I could muster, and said, "Thank you very much for letting me and Dylan stay, but it's time for us to leave now."

"But... why?" he asked, stepping out of bed and reaching for his discarded sweats. "You wanted last night to happen. We both did. You made it perfectly clear you weren't too drunk, or I never would have—"

"I know. I know what I said, and I don't blame you." I backed up another step toward the door.

"So, you're just gonna... leave?"

Another step. I was almost to the door. I nodded. "It's for the best. I need to take a step back and think about everything that's happened."

His expression fell. "I see."

I hated that look on his face almost as much as I hated the pain in my chest. But there was no help for it. I knew what I had to do.

Turning, I fled from his room.

15

Kaos

TINA AND DYLAN were leaving.

When they'd moved in, there'd been no discussion about an exit plan. Nobody knew how long they'd need to stay with me, but I'd assumed it'd be a few months. At least until the divorce was final. They'd only been under my roof for a week, barely enough time to get to know them, and now Tina looked like she couldn't get away from me fast enough.

I couldn't let them leave now.

Not like this.

Was she really that ashamed of what we did last night? Why? We were consenting adults finally scratching a relentless itch...

And who the fuck was I trying to kid? What we shared was a hell of a lot more than an itch. Being with her once hadn't scratched anything.

Then again, maybe it had. I'd had chicken pox as a child, and I remember it itching like the goddamn devil. Scratching didn't bring relief. It only broke open the sores and made me bleed. A fitting analogy since I stood there staring at the spot where Tina had just stood, feeling like she'd opened one of my veins and left me for dead.

She hadn't even looked me in the eyes.

Last night was the best goddamn night of my life, and I refused to let her label it a mistake.

Unfortunately, there was a hell of a lot more caught up in this mess than me and Tina. Dylan was a huge consideration, but I knew that kid was firmly on Team Kaos. I just had to figure out how to win his mom over. First, I needed to report the situation, though. Grabbing my cell phone, I called Emily, hoping like hell she was awake.

She answered on the third ring. "Mornin' Kaos. You're up early." She sounded way too chipper for the kind of day I was having

"Mornin'. Hope I didn't wake you."

"No, I was already up. What's going on? Is everything okay?" she asked.

"No. I... um... I fucked up, and I don't know what to do now."

"Just a second." In the background, I heard her muffled voice, followed by the sound of a door. "All right. You have my undivided attention. Tell me everything."

Confessing I'd gotten drunk and slept with the woman I was supposed to be protecting wasn't exactly on my bucket list. It made me feel like a fucking rookie taking my first tumble with a puck bunny who turned out to be the team owner's daughter. My ass would be on the chopping block, and I'd look like one hell of a motherfucking cliché. But this was no random tumble, and I needed Emily to understand that, so I laid it all out for her, glossing over the sordid details.

"It was consensual?" Emily asked.

I about dropped my goddamn phone. Apparently, some of those details were necessary after all. "Of course, it was consensual. What the fuck do you think I am?"

"Calm down, Kaos, it's nothing personal. I had to be sure."

Which made sense but was still pretty damn offensive. "We

were drinking, but neither of us were past the point of consent. We both wanted it," I assured her, but there was no way in hell I'd disclose that Tina had demanded I fuck her. Some details were sacred. "What I need to know is how the fuck do we get her to stay?"

Emily blew out a breath, sounding a little too resigned for my liking. "We don't."

"But that asshole's still out there gunnin' for her. She and Dylan are safer with me."

"Is that the only reason you want them there?" Emily asked, her voice full of challenge.

"No." I probably should have said more, but what I felt for Tina and Dylan had nothing to do with Emily, Ladies First, or the club. This was personal, and I wanted to keep the details close to my chest.

"I see," Emily said. "That's quite the predicament. Regardless, I'm glad you called to let me know she'll be going back to Elenore's."

"What?" Hadn't the woman been listening to a damn word I said? "She can't go back. Matt's still out there."

"Tina can go wherever she wants. She's not a prisoner, and you're not providing government-mandated protective custody. Our services are one-hundred percent voluntary, and if she wants to go back to Elenore's, that's her right. Hell, if she decided to go back to Matt, there wouldn't be a damn thing we could do about it. We offer a service, Kaos, not a prison cell. She's lived in one of those long enough."

Goddamn, that hit hard. "Yes, she has, but this is different. This is for her own safety. Can't they stay somewhere else? With you and the prez?"

"We don't have room at the house, and we're rarely home. They'd be alone most of the time, which is what we're trying to avoid. It'd make more sense for them to stay at the fire station, but Tina's already made it clear how she feels about that."

"There's gotta be someone else who can take them in." This was my fuckup and I refused to put them in danger because of it.

"I know your heart is in the right place, but if you try to force her to stay, she'll never forgive you."

"Force her?" I repeated, hating the very way the words tasted. "I would never force her to do shit." There had to be another option. An idea came to me, and I hurried to my closet to grab a bag. I'd pack a few days' worth of clothes and sleep in my Escalade in her parking garage. After this morning, she might not want my protection, but she was sure as shit going to get it.

"Last night wasn't a mistake, was it?" Emily asked. Before I could figure out how to answer that, she added, "At least, not for you. You love her, don't you? You love both of them."

I'd only known them for a week, so even thinking about love was asinine, but I didn't hesitate. No use lying. "I do. I know it doesn't make any damn sense, but they're..." Everything. The entirety of my whole fucking world had somehow been reduced to two people, and the idea of watching them walk out of my life was tearing me apart. "I can't lose them, Emily."

"I'm sure this move is only temporary," she assured me. "Give Tina some time and space. She's a smart, responsible woman. I'll call and check on her later to see if I can't angle her toward a more reasonable path. Regardless of how she feels about you, I'm confident she'll do what's right to protect Dylan."

That wasn't the motivation I was looking for. Sure, she and Dylan would always be safe with me, but I wanted her to stay for more. To stay because she couldn't stomach the idea of being away. Like all good Greek spawns, I'd taken philosophy in college, and a Socrates quote kept tugging at the back of my mind. 'Sometimes you put up walls not to keep people out, but to see who cares enough to break them down.' Matt had kicked down her walls and taken her prisoner. She'd escaped and built a fortress around herself.

If I was going to win her over, it'd take a hell of a lot more than a battering ram.

I needed to prove myself as an ally and convince her to carve me out a door.

Promising Emily I wouldn't do anything stupid, I disconnected the call, threw on a T-shirt, stuffed a few days' worth of clothes into my bag, and headed downstairs. Tina's bedroom door was open and she was inside, frantically stuffing clothes into a suitcase. The sight made me want to freak the fuck out and dump her bags so she couldn't leave me.

But that wasn't what she needed.

So instead, I set my pride aside and slipped into the room. "Hey, need some help?" I asked.

She startled and then stepped back like she expected me to attack. I held perfectly still and waited. When my words finally registered, her brow furrowed. "You... you want to help me?"

"I'm not gonna lie, Tina. I like having you and Dylan here. This past week has been great. Probably the best week of my life." I shook my head, chuckling. "I know that sounds like some bullshit line, but it's true. Hangin' out with you and Dylan, helpin' him with his homework, buildin' fuckin' blanket forts, sitting down to dinner like a family... that's all shit I never even knew I wanted for myself, but I'm sure gonna miss the hell out of it."

Her eyes softened marginally, but she stayed the course. Still watching me, she opened another dresser drawer and started transferring the contents into her suitcase. "You're a good guy, Darius. Any woman would be lucky to have that with you."

Any woman but the one I wanted, apparently. "Then why are you leaving?" I asked.

She blew out a breath. "Because I'm messed up, but I'm not... I don't wanna be a whore."

Huh? That was out of left field. "Did I do something to make you feel like one?" I asked.

She closed the drawer and deflated. Taking a seat on the bed, she faced me. "I'm not even divorced yet. I've only known you for a week, and I... We... That's not the kind of woman I want to be."

There was more to the story. There had to be. "Something happened to you, didn't it?"

She snorted and looked away. "Stuff happens to everyone."

I approached her slowly, sliding to my knees on the floor at her feet, making it clear through my body language that she held all the power. "Tell me. Please."

The remaining fire went out of her eyes and her brow furrowed. Minutes ticked by, but I didn't move. Didn't ask for more. She fidgeted and opened her mouth a few times, but nothing came out. Finally, she seemed to come to a decision and nodded. "Okay. Remember how I told you our dad wasn't around?"

Afraid to speak and make her withdraw again, I nodded.

"Mom... Mom was a struggle. At the time, we were living in Pomeroy. Are you familiar with the area?"

I shook my head.

"It's a small town of about fifteen hundred people. Approximately thirty miles west of the Idaho border."

"By Spokane?" I asked, trying to picture it in my head.

She wrinkled her nose. "About a hundred miles south of Spokane. In the middle of nowhere. Anyway, Mom had a lot of boyfriends." Her eyes glistened, and she looked away, blinking. "Boyfriends probably isn't the right word. She slept around. A lot. Everyone in the town knew it. People would always point at us and whisper. School was... bad. It's hard to make friends when your mom has slept with everyone's dad. When she died... people said she deserved it. They called her accident karma."

And Tina had been a teenager at the time. A teenager without a dad who'd just lost her mom. "Some people just suck ass."

She shrugged. "They were hurt. She hurt them. My mom wrecked homes and destroyed marriages. It was like she was on a mission to prove relationships were just a big farce." She blew out a breath. "I hated her for what she did to families. For what she did to me and Elenore."

"Under the circumstances, I'd say your hate was understandable, angel."

She frowned. "You called me that last night, when I was most definitely not behaving like an angel."

"I think you're a bit hard on yourself."

Again, her eyes glistened. She looked away, sniffling. "Can you blame me? Do you know what it's like to hear people call your mom a whore? I couldn't even argue with them. Instead, I vowed to be different. I made all these promises to myself... no sex until marriage, one husband for the rest of my life, no kids out of wedlock. I had all these great plans... all these ways to make sure I'd never turn out like my mom. My kids would never have to hear anyone call me the village bicycle."

Shit, that was harsh. I wanted to reach out to her—to comfort her—but didn't dare.

"Living with my uncle wasn't much better. He was so mad at mom for everything that he kept us at an arm's length. By the time I went to college I was so lonely." Her voice sounded hollow. "Pullman was more than an hour away from Pomeroy. There were almost thirty-thousand students on campus. People didn't know about my mom. It was... freeing. Then along came Matt, acting so sweet and caring, and I just wanted to be normal. I lost sight of all those promises I'd made to myself and let him lead me away from my dreams. I lost myself. And now, here you are. I'm not even legally divorced yet, and we... God." She ran a hand through her hair and met my gaze. "I can't lose myself again. I'm sorry, but I can't."

Understanding, I nodded, even as my world crashed down around me at her words. "Socrates once said, 'The greatest way to live with honor is to be what we pretend to be.' You are an angel, Tina. Matt clipped your wings for a time, but he can't keep you from flying indefinitely." The entire situation was fucked, and I had no idea how to fix it, but I had to try. Cupping her face in one hand, I said, "I'm not trying to change or cage you. I love you the way you are, and I want to help you fly."

Her breath hitched.

"I know you feel something for me, too. I'm not sorry for what we did last night, but I want you to be happy. If going back to your sister's is what you need right now, let me help you pack and drive you. I need to know you and Dylan are safe."

This time, she couldn't blink fast enough to keep a tear from sliding down her cheek. She hurriedly brushed it away and nodded. "Thank you."

"Of course. Whatever you need." I stood and went to wake up Dylan.

"I don't want to go back to Aunt El's," Dylan said, glaring at the open back door of my Escalade. His gaze shot to me, and hurt flooded his big hazel eyes. "Do you want us to leave, Kaos?"

There was no good way to answer. If I said no, that growing chip on his shoulder would be directed at his mom. But if I said yes, I'd crush him. This was so fucking hard. I swallowed back the lump forming in my throat and looked to Tina. Tears stood in her eyes, but determination kept them from falling.

"We'll discuss this later, Dylan. Get in the car," she said.

Giving me one last look, he announced, "This is stupid."

I agreed, but didn't say as much as he climbed in, strapped in, and immediately put his headphones on. Apparently, we were on ignore. Couldn't say I blamed the kid. With their suitcases loaded in the back, I opened Tina's door for her before rounding the SUV and getting behind the wheel. Adjusting my rearview mirror, I caught sight of Dylan staring straight ahead, headphones on, arms folded. Nothing about this had been my decision, but I couldn't shake the feeling that I was seriously letting him down.

If only I'd kept my dick in my pants.

Still, I didn't regret having sex with Tina. I couldn't. Not when I was desperately hoping for the chance to do it again. To do it every goddamn day for the rest of my life.

As we pulled out of the garage and headed down the street, she stared out the passenger side window like she couldn't bear to look at me. I didn't want to push her to talk, but the silence was suffocating. This felt like a game I'd played before. My team was down by a point with five seconds left on the clock.

Defeat was expected, which meant I had nothing to lose.

Time for a face-off.

"Thank you for telling me about your mom," I said.

That got Tina's attention. She turned to face me, her expression guarded. "You're welcome."

Silence stretched between us again. I wanted to say something, but I'd already taken a shot and needed to know I wasn't in this game alone. She was watching me. As I focused on the road, I could feel her gaze on the side of my face.

"I'm sorry about last night," she finally said, keeping her voice low. "I shouldn't have come upstairs."

I was doing my best to be understanding, but there was no way in hell I'd let her treat last night like a mistake. "Bullshit," I said.

She blinked, obviously confused by my outburst, but not dissuaded. "I drank a little too much, but I shouldn't have—"

"Bullshit," I repeated. "You can tell yourself it was the wine if that makes you feel better, but when you're talkin' to me, I'm gonna need you to be a little more honest. We've been racing toward that cliff since the day we met. Alcohol was just the vehicle we chose to drive us over the edge."

Clamping her mouth shut, she continued to stare at me.

"You wanted that to happen just as much as I did." I smacked my steering wheel for emphasis. "Needed it. And goddammit, it felt amazing."

Just thinking about last night was making things uncomfortable in my sweats. I adjusted. Her gaze shot to my crotch, and I gave myself a few strokes for good measure before smiling at her. "What's wrong, angel? Ready for some more?"

She startled and looked away. "Haven't you been listening to me?"

"Heard every word, but all your explainin' hasn't changed a thing about what I feel for you. If anything, knowing what you've overcome has only made me love you more."

"You barely know me," she snapped. Her head whipped to the backseat. "And keep your voice down. Dylan doesn't need to hear this."

"Yeah. Far be it for him to hear someone actually respecting his mom and treating her like she matters. You want to know what I think?" Without giving her time to respond, I continued, "I think you feel how strong and powerful this thing between us is, and it scares you. You have no idea what to do with a man who isn't trying to control you and manipulate your emotions, so you're pushing me away."

"I'm... I'm not even divorced yet."

"Another excuse."

Her eyes widened. "A very valid one."

I chuckled, but there was absolutely nothing funny about how I felt. "Bull. Shit. How much more are you gonna give that asshole?"

Confusion wrinkled her forehead. "This isn't about Matt. It's about me. I told you what my mom was like."

"You gave him nine years and a child. He's a sociopath... the kind of person who does fine as long as you play by his rules. The minute you stepped out of line and started thinking and doing for yourself, he snapped. He'd do whatever it took to get you back in line. And you let him—for nine years—and now that you've got a chance at happiness, you're allowing *him* to keep you down once again."

"My mom—"

"Isn't you!" I snapped. "You know, I'm having a hard time understanding why what your mom did was so wrong. So, she had a healthy sexual appetite. It takes two to tango, and if she was bumpin' uglies with married men... that's a choice those men made. But none of that matters, because you're nothing like her. You're an excellent mom and an incredible woman. You deserve to be happy. You laughed last night—really laughed—because you were with me, and I make you happy. You can lie to yourself all you want, but this thing between us... it's the real deal."

She chewed on her bottom lip for a minute, before glancing over her shoulder once again. "But Dylan... this will be confusing for him."

"Maybe for a minute." I shrugged. "But he's a smart kid. He knows what's up, and it'll be good for him to see you happy with a man who treats you right."

"I... I don't want to get stuck again. I have things I want to accomplish. Dreams I want to chase."

"Good. I want you to do whatever makes you happy."

Her eyes narrowed. "People aren't that self-sacrificing."

"You are!" I said, exasperated. "My parents are. Hell, even my shithead brothers would put aside their wants to make their wives and kids happy. Tina, I get that the only relationship you've ever been in has been with a narcissistic asshole who believes the world rotates around him, but most people are not like that. When you really love someone, their happiness *is* your happiness. I know you know this. I've seen the way you light up like a goddamn Christmas tree whenever Dylan's happy."

"It's too soon for me to start a relationship," she insisted.

"Who the fuck says?" I fired back. "What happens between me and you is our business. Nobody has the right to judge it, and I doubt that anyone even cares. You're not in Pomeroy anymore, angel."

"But your family—"

"Would be lucky to have you and Dylan be a part of it."

Her expression softened and she looked away.

"I'm not..." I huffed out a breath as I turned onto the street that would take us to Elenore's apartment. There was still so much to say, and I was running out of time. "I'm not tryin' to pressure you into anything. You know how I feel and what I want. I suspect that you feel and want the same things, but you need some time to sort things out. I get that. Take all the time you need. I'm not goin' anywhere."

Something about my tone must have given me away, because Tina's gaze crashed into mine. "What do you mean?" she asked.

"I packed a bag. I'll be camping out in Elenore's garage to make sure that motherfucker doesn't show his face."

I could tell the moment my words sunk in, because relief smoothed out the lines on her forehead and relaxed her jaw. "You don't have to do that," she said, her voice barely above a whisper.

"I know, but I want to. You and Dylan are important to me. It's worth a little discomfort to make sure you guys are okay." I pulled into the parking garage and slid into the spot Tina's car occupied before Tap drove it to the fire station. "Now, come on. Let's get you guys inside."

16

Tina

FOR THE FIRST time in my life, I was getting exactly what I asked for, and I absolutely hated it.

Arms loaded with our suitcases, Kaos led me and Dylan out of the parking garage, down the narrow walkway, and into Elenore's building. Since I had a key, we didn't have to call up to be let in. Unlocking the entry door, I turned to face Kaos.

"We can take it from here," I said, reaching for my bags. He'd already done so much, and this bizarre feeling of helplessness had suddenly grabbed ahold of me and wouldn't let go. I felt like I should do... something, but I had no idea what. Leaving him like this felt wrong, but I needed to sort myself out, and I didn't trust myself to do that while under the influence of his sweet words and incredible body.

"No. I'll see you all the way to the condo." He clutched the suitcase handle. "I need to make sure it's safe."

He'd accused me of having no idea what to do with a man who wasn't trying to control me and manipulate my feelings, and he was probably right. Maybe it was foolish to push him away, but I needed to assure myself that it was still an option. That he hadn't somehow trapped me and was planning to suffocate me for my own good like Matt always claimed to do.

Only I'd never felt remotely suffocated around Kaos.

My mind kept spinning in circles, making me feel indecisive and borderline certifiable. I'd made my decision and there'd be time to pick it apart later. For now, I needed to focus on putting one foot in front of the other, so I didn't do something stupid like beg him to take me back.

Or maybe leaving him was stupid.

No. I'd fallen too hard, too fast, and I needed to make sure I could still walk away when he showed his true colors.

Dylan hadn't said a word since before we'd left Kaos's house. Face pinched in a scowl, he walked past us both and headed for the elevator. I was grateful he didn't act up in front of Kaos, but feared my reprieve would end the instant our escort left.

Head dropped in defeat, I followed my son, and Kaos fell into step behind me. To an outsider, it probably looked like we were marching to our execution rather than heading to my sister's. Nobody said a word during the elevator ride. The somber silence stretched all the way to my sister's unit. Finally, I unlocked the door and reached for my luggage. Releasing the bags where he stood, Kaos dropped to his knees, grabbing Dylan by the shoulders to get his undivided attention.

"You asked me if I wanted you to leave," he said, his voice raspy and full of emotion. "No. I don't want either of you to leave." His gaze strayed to me for a moment before returning to Dylan. "But sometimes adults have to figure shit out. We're not perfect, and it can be difficult to trust after we've been hurt. Your mom and I… we're doin' the best we can. I don't want you givin' her any shit about it. You hear me?"

Dylan's gaze cut to me before he nodded.

"She and I have stuff to figure out, but that's got nuthin' to do with you. No matter what, I'll be here for you. Whatever you need."

Again, Kaos's gaze met mine. "Both of you. All you have to do is call."

My heart squeezed, and I wondered for the hundredth time if I was doing the right thing. Then again, this move didn't have to be permanent. Maybe some time away would help me get my head on straight so I could figure out what I wanted. From Kaos and from myself. Maybe once the divorce was final, I wouldn't feel like such a whore every time I looked at him.

Dylan's eyes flooded with tears, but he blinked them away. "But I'll miss you, Kaos."

A sad smile played on the man's lips. "I'll miss you, too, Mayhem."

That put a genuine smile on my sweet boy's face.

"But I'll be around," Kaos assured him. "You're not getting rid of me that easily."

"Will you still coach me?" Dylan asked.

Kaos looked to me, and I gave him a slight nod. There was no way I'd keep Dylan from him. Ever. Positive male role models were in short supply, and if Kaos wanted to step up, I would welcome the help.

"Absolutely," he replied, mussing Dylan's hair. "I wouldn't miss the opportunity to work with you for all the cereal in America. Now, why don't you head inside and let me say goodbye to your mom."

Dylan hugged him.

The sight of that big, sweet, hunk of a man hugging my sad, confused boy tugged at every one of my heartstrings. The backs of my eyes stung, and I had to avert my gaze so I didn't cave. When the two of them pulled apart, Dylan's cheeks were wet. He swiped at the moisture, promised to see Kaos later, frowned at me, and headed inside.

But at least he hadn't thrown a fit.

Kaos stood and faced me.

"Thank you," I said, taking the handle of my suitcase from him. "For everything."

He shook his head, closing the distance between us until we were almost touching. "You don't have to thank me. I wasn't bullshittin' you when I told you this was the best week of my life. I enjoyed every minute of it." A frown turned down his lips. "Well, until you said you wanted to leave. That sucked ass."

I could feel his body heat, and smell mint on his breath. I wanted nothing more than to lean against him and let his strong, powerful arms protect me from the world.

But I needed to do this for me. Needed to make sure I could walk away, that I hadn't somehow managed to trap myself with another man. I stepped back, reaching for the door.

I half expected him to stop me, but he didn't.

"I'll be close if you need me," he said, simply.

"Thanks again." The words sounded so lame and insignificant, but they were all I had to offer.

He let me go. I walked right past him and into the condo, closing the door behind me.

When I looked through the peep hole, Kaos stood in the hallway, exactly where I'd left him. He gave the door a longing look that threatened to squeeze the life out of my heart. Then he dropped his head and ambled back toward the elevator.

I stood there, staring, both relieved and disappointed to see him leave. He'd made it clear he wanted us to be together, but he didn't guilt or beg me to come back. There were no threats, no name-calling, no violence.

He just... left.

And the sight of his retreating back made me realize how badly I'd effed this all up. He was a good guy, so he was giving me the space I'd asked for, but that wasn't what I needed.

I needed him.

Before Kaos came into my life, I was healing. But he'd empowered me to heal faster, better. He'd given me the strength to put my foot down and say no. And then he'd respected my decision.

And I'd been willing to give it all up for some screwed up sense of propriety.

Thankfully, Kaos had godlike patience and was willing to wait for me to see the truth for myself. We were meant to be together. I liked who I was when I was with him. I liked who he was.

No, I loved him.

The realization felt like it broke some kind of chain deep inside me that had kept me tethered to the little girl who hated the way people laughed and pointed at her. I no longer cared what anyone thought about the fact my divorce wasn't even final yet. I had a chance to finally be happy—for my son to finally be happy—and I was taking it.

Dylan was nowhere in sight. I searched until I found him back in his old room, sitting on the bed with his back to the door. Circling around to join him, I sat and draped my arm over his shoulders. I half expected him to pull away, but he did the opposite, leaning against me as he wiped tears from his face. Tears that were my fault because I'd been too stupid to see what was right in front of me.

"I love you, baby," I said.

"I love you, too, Mom." His voice hitched, and it felt a lot like sandpaper running over my heart.

"I've loved you from the moment I found out you were growing in my belly. I didn't have a very good mom, and I wanted to be the best mom ever for you. I made all these promises to always do the right thing to keep you safe and happy. But I'm not perfect, and sometimes, I don't know what the right thing is. I used to think staying with your dad was the right thing, but it wasn't, was it."

"My dad is not a good man."

This was the first time he'd ever said anything negative about his father. The words hung in the air like poisonous gases. I wanted to swat them away, but I needed to know how deadly they were first. "Why do you say that?" I asked.

He looked up at me, his hazel eyes so honest and open. "You didn't fall down the stairs, Mom."

The foundation of who I was as a mother and protector cracked. "Who told you?"

"Nobody. I'm not stupid."

I was floored. All this time, I'd been trying to protect him from the truth, and he already knew it. He'd hinted to that knowledge at Kaos's, but now... now I knew for sure. I'd sacrificed so my boy could be happy, but he knew what was up all along. I'd been so... so stupid.

"How would you feel about me... dating Kaos?" I asked, wincing at the way that sounded. But I didn't know how else to put it. Dylan had proven how observant he could be, and this decision would affect him as much as it did me. If I was going back to Kaos—if we were truly going to make this work—I needed my son's blessing.

Dylan seemed to mull it over for a few minutes before asking, "Like you'd be his girlfriend?"

The title seemed too juvenile for what I wanted to share with Kaos, but I nodded. "Yes."

"Would he be my dad?"

"You have a dad."

"But what if I *want* Kaos to be my dad?"

Gah. That was a tough question. "That's a conversation you need to have with him. I just need to know if you're okay with me dating him."

"Yeah. I like him, and he seemed really sad about us leaving. Can we go back to his house now?"

I chuckled. "You really want to?"

"Yes." Hope widened Dylan's eyes as he jumped up from the bed. "Can we? Please?"

How could I say no to such excitement? "Yes. But first, let me go talk to Aunt El. Have you seen her?"

He shook his head, grabbing the bags he'd left by the door. Before I left, he stopped me. When I turned around, his gaze met mine.

"You are a good mom," he said. "You're just tryin' to do the best you can."

God, I loved him so much. My sweet boy was back, the child he'd been before all this garbage with his father went down. Kaos had been great for me, but he'd been stellar for my child. Hugging Dylan as tightly as I could, I wiped away tears and pulled myself together.

"Thank you," I whispered against his forehead before I released him to go tell my sister hello and goodbye.

Elenore wasn't usually one to sleep in, even on the weekends, but since I'd seen her car in the parking garage, I knew she had to be here somewhere. Her schedule had been busy this past week, and I'd spoken to her very little since I'd moved out. I couldn't wait to tell her my news about Kaos, so like any good sister would, I didn't bother to knock when I reached her bedroom door. I just barged right in, calling out her name.

Elenore was there, but my sister wasn't alone.

A wave of tattooed flesh crested over the bed and I realized... Oh my god, I realized it was a man. And she'd just shoved him out of the bed. His naked body hit the floor and he cried out a curse. Elenore grabbed the covers and pulled them up to her chin, but not before I realized she was naked, as well.

Covering my eyes with my hands, I turned away. "El?" I asked, shocked by what I'd seen and needing to know that she was okay. Had he been attacking her?

"It's not what it looks like," she hurried to say.

Then what the heck was it? "Are you... okay?"

"Yes." She huffed out a laugh. "Just stupid."

That didn't make me feel any better. Pretty sure I'd recognized the man she'd just flung from her bed, I asked, "Is that... Rabbit?" I'd only met him once, when he showed up with Kaos and Tap to get me and Dylan out of here, but Rabbit was the kind of man who made an impression.

"Hey, Tina, how you doin'?" Rabbit asked, confirming my suspicions.

"She'd probably be doing better if you'd get dressed," Elenore snapped.

Rabbit chuckled. "What's wrong, babe? Don't wanna share me with your sister?"

"You're diabolical."

"Why thank you."

What in the heck was going on here? "I... I think I should come back later." I took a step back, preparing to make my escape.

"No, don't go. Rabbit was just leaving." Elenore said.

"Like hell I was," Rabbit said. "I won that bet, and I'm not goin' anywhere until you pay up. Although, of course, I might be willin' to go double or nuthin'."

What the actual insanity...? "Okay. Well, um... call me... later. When you can talk." And answer questions, because I had so many of those filtering through my head. Not to mention the images that kept promising to scar me for life. My God, had I seen a flash of metal coming from his...

No.

Refusing to think about that, I stepped out to a chorus of Elenore's pleas for me to stay and Rabbit's maniacal laughter. Closing the door behind me—because Dylan definitely did not need to see whatever was going down in my sister's bedroom—I retrieved my son from his room and hastily shooed him down the hallway.

"I wanna say bye to Aunt El," he said, dragging his feet as we passed her door.

"Yeah, no. That's not gonna happen. Aunt El has..." clearly lost her mind, "company."

Raised voices came from the other side of the door.

"Are they fighting?" Dylan asked, sounding concerned.

"They're..." crazy. The whole situation was insane. My straitlaced, brilliant scientist sister was sleeping with... Rabbit? "Ironing out their differences." And my sister was nothing like me. She'd told me she was okay, and I believed her. She was always honest, and she had a history of marching out of any situation she didn't want to be in.

If Rabbit was here, I had no doubt Elenore had invited him.

I shuddered against the thought, practically shoving Dylan out the door and grabbing my suitcases along the way.

"You're acting weird," he said.

"I'm just anxious to get back to Kaos's." And I was pretty sure my sister was off her rocker, but Dylan had seen enough, and he didn't need to bear witness to that insanity. I'd have to tell Kaos about it, and maybe he could send Tap to check out the situation.

But all thoughts of my sister's predicament fled as we hurried out of the building and turned down the path that would lead to the parking garage, almost running smack into my worst nightmare.

Matt.

17

Tina

A NASTY, SCORNFUL smile played on Matt's lips as his gaze took in me, Dylan, and our luggage. "Exactly where are you two off to in such a hurry?" he asked.

Icy fingers of dread threatened to cripple me even as my hand went to my pocket, searching for my phone. Matt zeroed in on what I was doing and opened his jacket just enough to give me a glimpse of the handle of a gun holstered at his side. I looked to Dylan, hoping he hadn't seen it, but his eyes were wide as saucers and laser-focused on the weapon.

"Dad, why do you have a gun?" he asked.

Matt's smile turned smug. "Because my wife has forgotten her place and needs a little reminder of who she is and what her duties are. You miss me, Tina?"

Miss him? His presence made my stomach curdle. I wanted to throw up.

Matt sidled up next to me, and something hard pressed into my side. The gun. Had to be. He was pressing it to my side in a silent threat. I met his gaze, and the hate that stared back at me turned my blood to ice. I had no doubt he'd use that gun in a hot minute. The look he was giving me... it was like he was begging for an excuse to fire. Desperate, I scanned the area for help, but the little walkway we stood on between the condo building and the parking garage was off the street and secluded by trees and bushes. Matt had found us in the most inconvenient place. The building only had about a dozen residents, and unless one of them happened by, I was screwed.

Panic threatened to squeeze the air out of my lungs, but one look at Dylan's terrified face forced me to take a breath. I was Mom. Moms didn't get the luxury of panic attacks or mental breakdowns, especially not while being held at the business end of a gun in front of their kid. I couldn't freak out. I had to think and figure a way out of this nightmare.

My phone vibrated against my hip. Probably Elenore calling to explain whatever was happening in her bedroom. Maybe if I bought some time, she'd get dressed and come down here to see if she could catch us. Better yet, maybe she'd send Rabbit. Kaos was in the garage. The entrance was only a few yards away, but the distance separating us seemed like miles. Continents, even.

"How... how've you been?" I asked, trying to get Matt talking, hoping I could remind him that I was a good person.

The question only seemed to enrage him further. "How the fuck do you think I've been? My wife and son vanished off the face of the planet. I found your car parked beside some... some motorcycle gang hangout."

I needed to deescalate the situation. Quickly. So, like always, I accepted all the blame. "I'm sorry. I... I messed up. I shouldn't have left."

He yanked on my arm, jerking me against him and digging the gun deeper into my side. I gasped at the sharp pain.

"No, you damn well shouldn't have."

"But you found us." I tried to give his bruised ego a little boost. "How'd you find us?"

"I'm resourceful."

I didn't ask him to elaborate, didn't play his game, because I knew the chance to brag would eat him alive until he gave in to it. And Matt didn't disappoint. Huffing out a breath, he finally admitted what he'd done. "Paid someone to install a hidden camera by the door. Figured you'd show back up and I've been monitoring the feed on my phone, and I just happened to catch you two walking into the building with..." His eyes narrowed. "Who the fuck was that guy? Pretty sure I've seen him before."

While I was still trying to figure out an answer that wouldn't result in my immediate death, Dylan piped up with, "My hockey coach."

As far as answers went, that wasn't a bad one. Far less damning than any I could think of. At least Matt hadn't realized Kaos was the one who'd served him divorce papers. That probably wouldn't go well for any of us. Relieved, I nodded enthusiastically.

"You're letting Dylan play hockey?" Matt asked, his tone suspicious.

Due to my desire to keep my son from danger, I could fully understand Matt's skepticism. "Yep. I did some research, and it turns out team sports are good for kids."

He snorted. "No. You're not playin' hockey, Dylan. That's not even an American sport. Basketball's where it's at. You wanna play a team sport? I'll sign you up for basketball. You really should have asked me first, Kristina."

My mother had named me Kristina after herself. I'd gone by Tina since the day I decided I didn't want to be anything like her. Matt knew I hated the name, and he used it like a weapon... reminding me of where I came from. Of whose daughter I was. Usually, it served as an effective whip to keep me in line, but today, it just pissed me off. I was so tired of his games and manipulations. How dare he show up at my sister's with a gun! In front of Dylan, no less! Gritting my teeth, I let the anger fuel me and burn away the panic that wanted to settle in as he tugged me forward, angling toward a trodden path that veered off the walkway.

My gut clenched, and I knew if he got us out of here, I'd never survive.

"Where are you taking us?" I asked.

"Home. Where you belong."

Doubtful. He might take Dylan home, but my body would probably end up elsewhere. "That's not our home. Not anymore. What are you gonna do? Hold me prisoner?"

He backhanded me.

I barely registered the movement of his hand before my face exploded in pain. Head whipping around, I would have lost my balance and ended up in the bushes if Dylan's little hands hadn't landed on my back to keep me vertical.

"Run," I whispered, desperate to save him. Kaos said he'd be in the garage. If Dylan could get to him, he'd be safe. Kaos would never let anything happen to my boy.

Instead of obeying, Dylan's eyes hardened. He stepped around me, squaring up with his dad. "Do not hit my mom," he ground out.

Ignoring him, Matt glared at me. "What the fuck did you do? Turn my own son against me?'

"No," Dylan said, refusing to be ignored. "You did that yourself."

Rage flared in Matt's eyes. Seeing the danger Dylan was in, I tried to push him behind me, but he resisted, widening his stance.

"You're nuthin' but a... a nar... narcissistic asshole!" he shouted at his dad.

Oh no.

Dread felt like a weight in my stomach as Matt whipped out his gun, sneering at our child. "I don't know what the fuck kind of lies your mom has been feeding you, but you do not get to talk to me like that, boy. I'm your fucking father!"

"I don't want you to be," Dylan said, his voice barely a whisper as the truth of his words crashed into him. He used to idolize this man. He wanted to be just like him, and now, he acknowledged his dad for what he truly was, and my heart broke for my kid.

Matt leveled the gun at Dylan.

At my sweet boy. At my world.

Dylan had never talked back to him before, and now... Matt had clearly lost his mind.

I couldn't let him hurt Dylan.

Fear and rage for my son drove me to act without thinking. Shoving Dylan into the bushes, I dove for Matt, tackling him as the gun went off.

Kaos

Pulling my iPad out of my bag, I settled into the driver's seat of the Escalade, preparing to check my email and maybe play a game or two. I'd given Tina a lot to think about, and was hoping she'd have a nice little chat with her sister, realize she missed me as much as I missed her, and then call to let me know she was ready to go home.

Home.

It was strange how I'd never really considered my house home before. Home had always been the place I'd grown up, the house my parents now entertained their horde of grandchildren in. My house was where I slept and kept all my shit, but it had never felt like a home.

Not until Tina and Dylan came along and made it feel that way.

Then again, maybe the house wasn't home. Maybe they were, because I couldn't imagine going back there without them. It would go back to feeling like a house, all cold, lonely, and quiet. I didn't want to live there without them.

My calf started cramping.

If I was going to start skating regularly with Dylan, I'd need to start taking potassium and get better about stretching. Getting old was some shit. I kicked out my leg, but the cramp only intensified. Setting my iPad down, I got out of the SUV and started pacing. The physical pain was a nice distraction from the ache inside my chest, and I moved slowly, in no hurry to work it out.

When the pain finally subsided, I climbed back into my rig and answered a few emails and checked stock prices, wondering how Tina and Dylan were doing. Would Elenore try to talk some sense into her? Or would she welcome her back with open arms, relieved that Tina refused to take a chance on me.

Fuck!

It was all I could do to keep my ass in that garage when I wanted nothing more than to march back up to Elenore's and demand that Tina and Dylan come home.

My phone rang. Hope made me snatch it up before the first ring ended, but disappointment leveled me out when Morse's name flashed across the screen.

"Hello?" I answered.

"Hey Kaos. I see you're in Elenore's building's garage," Morse said into my ear. "Everything okay?"

Emily must not have gotten the chance to fill him in yet. Eyeing the camera that he no doubt watched me from, I nodded. "It will be." I sounded a hell of a lot more confident than I felt, but I didn't want to get into all the shit that had gone down.

"Are Tina and Dylan inside?" Morse asked.

I nodded, and then realized that even if he was watching me, he probably couldn't make out what I was doing in my rig. "Yeah. You didn't see us go in?"

"No. I had some errands to run this morning, and just got into the office. We're checking the feeds now."

"Morse!" Hound shouted in the background. "Camera C."

I tensed, wondering what the hell Camera C was and why Hound sounded like he was about to shit himself.

"Fuck. Matt's there," Morse said, his words clipped. "By the front door. He's got Tina and Dylan."

"What?" His words refused to register, but my body reacted instantly. I was out the door before he could answer.

"Get there, Kaos. Fuckin' get there now!"

Still confused, I sprinted for the exit, cursing how far away Tina's parking spot was.

"That's a... Shit. He has a gun. He's aimin' at the fuckin' kid!"

Pushing myself harder than I ever had in my life, I darted around the corner. A blur caught my attention. Dylan. Flying through the air?

POW!

The loud, explosive pop of gunfire made my ears ring.

Dylan landed in the bushes.

I started to run for him, but beyond him, Tina and Matt hit the ground. Landing on top of him with a bone-jarring thump, she was fighting. Swinging, her hands swiped at the gun, knocking it out of his hand. It slid just out of his reach.

"Bitch!" Matt shouted.

He balled up his fist, and I rushed them. I heard the fleshy thud of his fist finding purchase, and her head bobbed backwards. But she kept swinging.

A strange mix of pride and rage filled me as I reached them. Matt's hand stretched for the gun, but I stomped on it. He screamed. The bastard must have been too busy to realize I was there, and it took him a moment to register what was causing the pain. His gaze met mine, and his eyes widened as I lifted Tina off of him. Flailing arms and legs wildly, she somehow managed to land a kick between his legs.

Matt doubled over, spitting out curses and threats as he cupped his crotch.

"I got you, angel," I said, setting her down.

She stilled, and then turned to look at me. Then her eyes widened with terror as she looked toward the bushes. "Dylan!"

She dove for her boy while I kicked Matt's gun well out of his reach.

The bastard's gaze met mine, and he must have seen his death in my eyes, because he started scooting back and stammering about how his wife was responsible and if she'd only done what he told her to, this could have all been prevented.

At least, that's what I imagined he said.

In reality, his lips moved, but I'd slipped into that space where sound was inconsequential. All that existed was red hot rage.

I roared.

Fucking roared.

It was the only response I could think of to get him to shut the fuck up. And he really needed to stop talking, because my restraint was in threads, and if he said one more derogatory thing about Tina, I was going to rip his motherfucking vocal cords out through his asshole.

Matt clamped his mouth closed. Eyes wide as saucers, he watched me.

Morse was screaming my name.

It snapped me out of whatever trance I'd been in. Realizing the phone was still in my hand, I held it to my ear. "I'm busy. I'll have to get back to you."

"You're in the camera's line of sight. I don't care what the fuck you do to that piece of shit, but if you do it where there's video evidence, Emily will lose her shit. Be smart. Drag his ass five feet toward the garage. There's a blind spot there."

It took a minute for Morse's words to sink in, and when they finally did, I let out some deranged sounding cackle. God, it was good to have brothers who had my back.

Grabbing ahold of Matt by his fucking shirt, I dragged him five feet down the path and put the phone back up to my ear. "This good?"

"Yeah, brother. You're clear. Have fun, but try not to kill him."

The line went dead.

Tina was helping Dylan to his feet.

"Is he okay?" I asked.

She nodded, and I felt her relief down to my very soul. We could have lost him. The stupid fucking piece of shit lying at my feet had taken a shot at him. Tina's face was swollen and the area around her eye was already starting to turn colors. She squeezed Dylan to her side, glaring at Matt.

I also felt her anger. It fueled mine, and if I didn't let it out, I'd explode.

"Good. The Escalade's unlocked. Go get in it and call the cops."

Matt needed to be dealt with, but it wasn't a thing I wanted either of them to see. Tina hesitated, no doubt worried about the consequences I'd face, but Dylan grabbed her hand and started walking toward the parking garage. I gave him a nod of approval, and he returned the gesture.

"That kid is more of a man then you'll ever be," I spat at Matt.

He started babbling again, throwing around accusations and calling Tina all sorts of messed-up shit. "You fuckin' my slut now?" he shouted at me. "Like my sloppy seconds, do you?"

I waited until she and Dylan were out of sight, and then I shut his ass up with a quick jab to the collar bone.

Matt's eyes widened in pain.

Pussy. It wasn't even hard. Barely more than a love tap. I was just getting started. "Like *that*, motherfucker?" I asked. "No. That's right. You only like beating on people smaller than you. Bet you've never even raised your fist to a man before, have you? Well, come on now. Here's your chance." I stepped back, giving him time and room to get up.

Eyeing me, he started to stand, but changed his mind and took a cheap shot at my nuts instead. Thankfully, the bastard was slow, and I easily evaded his fist. I'd given him a chance to fight fair, and he'd gone for my nuts like a goddamn pussy. Pissed, I kicked him in the ribs.

Grunting, Matt writhed to the side.

"Unlike you, I derive no joy from kickin' people when they're down. Get your pathetic ass up before I fuckin' make you."

Centering Kaos

When he finally got to his feet, I took a swing at his left eye. "How does that feel? You like that shit? I saw the pictures, by the way. Saw what you did to her. I memorized every cut, every bruise, you gave her, and I've been waiting for this moment." The moment I'd get to do the same to him. "After all, if you did it to her, it's only fair that someone does it to you."

Fear must have finally sunk in, because the piece of shit took off running.

He only made it about three steps before I caught his ass and dragged him back. Then I let him experience what an uppercut to the jaw felt like. His throat was next. Wrapping my hands around his neck, I squeezed until the motherfucker was gasping for air. Releasing him, I used his ribs as a punching bag. Next, I gave him a good old-fashioned dead leg before kicking him in the kidney and punching my way up and down both of his arms. The fucker didn't just stand there and take it. No, he somehow managed to land two punches to my chest and a jab to my throat.

At some point during the fight, Rabbit appeared, leaning against the wall to watch. Matt begged him for help, but a vein started throbbing in my club brother's forehead as he bared his teeth like some kind of feral cat. "Oh, I'm not here to help you, dumbass. I'm here to make sure nobody intervenes. Goddamn woman beater." He spat. "You get tired, Kaos, you tag me in. I'd like a piece of this motherfucker, too."

Not fucking likely. This asshole was all mine. Matt took a desperate swing at me, and I stepped inside and jabbed him in the gut for his trouble.

"What's wrong, ass wipe?" Rabbit called out with a chuckle. "You never fight a man before?"

By the time the cops arrived, I felt like I'd delivered the type of justice an ass wipe like Matt could understand. Dropping to my knees, I put my hands behind my back and let them cuff me. I'd never been arrested before, but I knew enough not to incriminate myself.

Emily was waiting at the police station when we arrived. She took one look at the damage I'd done to Matt and shook her head.

But I caught the way her eyes smiled.

My official statement was that I saw a man take a shot at a child and I told the woman to call the cops while I attempted to make a citizen's arrest. When the suspect resisted, I used force.

The booking officer stared at me, unblinking. "Don't you think that force was a little excessive?"

I shrugged. "Oh, that's not all from me. The son-of-a-bitch is clumsy. He must have fallen down a flight of stairs."

"Sure did," Rabbit chimed in from another officer's desk, where he was giving his statement, vouching for me. "Saw the whole thing."

18

Kaos

MY KNUCKLES WERE bruised and all cut to shit, but it was the most rewarding pain I'd ever felt in my life. Taking Matt's twisted, fucked-up sense of power away from him was satisfying on a whole new level. Given the chance between winning the Stanley Cup and grinding that motherfucker's face into the cement, there was no doubt in my mind which option I'd choose.

It was kind of wild how far my priorities had shifted.

Beating the shit out of Matt would have been worth jail time, but Emily worked her magic. Tina, Dylan, Rabbit, and Elenore all gave their statements, and I was released and told not to leave town. That wasn't a problem, since everything I wanted was in Seattle.

Matt was being held without bail, and Tina and Dylan were finally safe to live their lives without him.

Since Tina had the Escalade, I hadn't expected her and Dylan to stick around and wait for me to be released, but when I stepped into the waiting room, they were there. Dylan ran to me and threw his arms around my waist. Seeming to remember he was too cool for that touchy-feely bullshit, he released me and shook my hand instead.

"Do we get to go home now?" he asked.

The way he said it gave me pause. Was he talking about my place? I looked to Tina. She nodded, tears pooling in her eyes.

Mussing his hair, I nodded. "Yeah. Nothing would make me happier than to take you home. I'm starving. You hungry?"

He grinned up at me. "I'm a growing boy, Kaos. I'm always hungry."

Chuckling, I headed for the door. Tina joined us along the way, her expression concerned.

"I'm sorry," she said. "About earlier. We never should have left your house."

"Home," I corrected, holding my arm out to the side. She hesitated for only a moment before taking the invitation and tucking her body against mine. My arm felt good draped over her shoulders. It felt right. "You had some shit to work out," I said. "What I don't understand is how Matt got to you."

"Matt said he installed a camera by the door, and he caught us going in on the feed. We were coming back out. I'd realized how stupid I was being and I..." She glanced at Dylan and corrected herself. "We wanted to come... home."

Squeezing her against me, I kissed the top of her head. "You have no idea how happy it makes me to hear you say that."

I drove, and Tina called for a pizza. The delivery man arrived at the house just moments after we did. We stuffed our faces, and then dragged our asses into the family room to watch *The Goonies*. Tina cleaned the cuts on my hands, and I filled a baggie with ice for her eye. We must have looked like quite the pair. By the time we got situated on the sofa, Dylan was out cold. I turned off the movie, scooped him up, and carried him to bed before leading Tina into my room. She gave me a little side-eye, but I pleaded the case that we were both tired, I wanted to talk—only talk—and after the day we'd had, I needed her close to me. Needed to keep reassuring myself she was safe.

"Dylan called Matt a narcissistic a-hole," she said, making herself comfortable on my bed. She was fully clothed, and I was fine with that. I hadn't been lying when I'd said I only wanted to talk. We had some catching up to do, and I'd learned my lesson and didn't want to rush back into something she might regret.

Keeping my sweats and T-shirt on, I slid onto the bed beside her, smiling. "That kid's wise beyond his years."

"Wise?" She gaped at me. "I think the word you're looking for is devious. He must have listened in on our conversation."

"Can you blame him?" I fired back. "The adults in his world keep fucking up and he needed to know what was going on. I'm damn proud of him for the way he stood up for you. If he was a little older, I'd buy him a car."

"He could have been killed." Her voice hitched, and I realized she was barely holding herself together.

"Yeah, but he wasn't." I extended my arm up over her head. She scooted in, snuggling against my side. Right where she belonged. It felt so goddamn good and natural. Complete.

She let out a shuddering breath.

"He's okay," I assured her. "And Emily says that fucker's gonna be locked up for a while. Even if he does get out, there's no way in hell a judge will grant him visitation. Not after today."

"Yeah, he really screwed up this time, didn't he?"

"No, angel." I chuckled. "He done fucked up. Call it what it is." When she didn't reply, I looked down at her. "Some situations require stronger words, but you don't ever really cuss, do you?"

"I try really hard to be a lady."

Unable to help myself, I chuckled at that. "You don't think ladies cuss?" I couldn't wait to tell Carisa. That woman could make a sailor blush.

"I'm not judging anyone who does," Tina hurried to say. "It's just been a thing for so long."

Reading between the lines, I realized what she meant. "Matt didn't like it."

She didn't confirm, but she didn't need to.

I swiped the hair back from her forehead and planted a kiss there. "That piece of shit no longer holds any power over you. You checked his ass like a goddamn defenseman. I gotta tell you, it was kinda hot to see the momma bear come out, all claws and teeth, protecting her cub."

Tina's laugh vibrated against my side. It was nice hearing her laugh after all she'd been through today.

"You're a badass now, so I need you to do something for me."

"Okay...?" She sounded hesitant.

"Tell me to fuck off."

She shook her head, giggling. "I'm not telling you that."

"Yes, you are. It's important practice for our future. I'm only a man and I'm gonna screw up, angel. We both need to know that you have the power to tell me to fuck off when I do." When she didn't immediately comply, I hooked my finger under her chin and tugged it up until she met my gaze. "Tell me to fuck off."

Her eyes searched mine and the laughter died on her lips at whatever she saw. Finally, she nodded. "Fuck off, Darius." Her voice was barely more than a whisper, and one lone tear slid down her cheek.

I swiped at it with my thumb, understanding how important this moment was for her. And... it was kind of hot. Never thought I'd be turned on by a woman telling me to pound pavement, but here we were. Seemed like I found everything Tina said and did sexy. "Good. Louder."

Squaring her shoulders, she maintained eye contact. "Fuck off." This time, there was a little glimmer of mischief in her eyes.

I grinned. "Give me more, angel."

Emboldened, she sat up. "Fuck all the way off. Fuck off until you can't fuck any further, and then fuck off some more."

Goddamn, she was everything. Looking proud as a rooster, she stared at me. Resting my hand against the unbruised side of her face, I drew my thumb over her lips.

"That's a whole lot of fuckin', angel," I said.

Her eyes liquefied and she let out a breathy little sound that went straight to my cock.

"Don't look at me like that, badass. No sex tonight. I promised. Now, lie back down here beside me and tell me how much you missed my sexy ass."

Chuckling, she collapsed, tucking herself back against my side. "You're ridiculous. We were only apart for like a half hour."

"And then I was interrogated and did several hours of hard time in the slammer."

She rubbed circles on my belly with her fingertip. "You poor baby."

"I know, right? There was this one guy in there who looked like he'd taken the mall Santa gig a little too far. Smelled like piss and cheap whiskey. He kept checkin' out my ass, and I feared for my bootyhole."

She gave me a little mock gasp. "Your bravery astounds me."

"As it should. I'm very fucking astounding." I chuckled a moment before sobering. "All kiddin' aside, you really did scare me when you left. And for what it's worth, I did miss you. You know, that's not something they say in Greece."

"Oh? What do the Greek say?" she asked.

"*Mou leipeis*. It translates closer to you are missing from me. That's what it felt like when I dropped you and Dylan off, angel. Like a part of me was missing. I know it wasn't long, but I'd like very much for us to never do that again."

Wrapping her arm around my midsection, she gave me a squeeze. "You're so... unexpected, Darius."

I liked it when she called me by my given name. It sounded almost like a purr on her soft, plump lips. "What do you mean?" I asked.

"You're a hockey-playing Army veteran who quotes Socrates,

sings Hawaiian music lyrics, always knows what to say, and is great with my son."

And she was good for my ego. Patting her hand, I said, "You forgot the sex god part."

She laughed, but didn't disagree. I took that as a win.

We stayed like that for hours, just talking and getting to know each other better. The more I learned about her, the more it reaffirmed that this woman was it for me. At some point, we must have dozed off, because Tina's phone alarm startled us both awake. Throwing back the covers, she rolled out of my bed, almost smacking her head on the nightstand.

"Whoa. Where do you think you're goin'?" I asked. The woman looked dead on her feet. She went to knuckle her eyes, but winced at the pain. Just looking at the bruises on her face made me wish bail had been set for Matt. I'd be tempted to bail his ass out so I could beat the shit out of him again.

"I need to wake Dylan up for school."

"No, you don't."

Her eyes narrowed at me. "Do I need to start telling you to fuck off already?"

My God, I'd created a little wildcat. Laughing, I threw up my hands to shield myself from her ferocious glare. "No ma'am. But the kid just rescued his mom and gave a statement to lock up his dad. I think he deserves a day off."

Deflating, she collapsed back on the bed. "Yeah. You're probably right."

"Wow. I don't mean to brag or anything, but you're the second woman who's told me that this week."

Her head snapped around and she glared at me. "What other woman are you talking to?"

Even her jealousy was hot as fuck. My cock took notice, springing to life and encouraging me to show Tina she was the only woman for me. She'd ditched her bra some time during the night, because the natural form of her breasts got my attention quick. I tugged her over the bed until she straddled me. Tucking her long brown locks behind her ears, I grinned up at her. "Carisa, angel. Nothin' for you to get all worked up about. Although, I kinda like this side of you."

"Oh." Her brow furrowed. "I wasn't getting worked up. I just—"

"Yes, you were. And I don't blame you. I'm a fuckin' beefcake." I rolled my hips, letting her feel how hard she made me. "But you don't have to worry. I'm *your* beefcake."

Her eyes softened.

Grabbing her hands, I tugged her down until she was lying on top of me. Our lips pressed together in a slow, sensual kiss. I probably should have brushed my teeth before pulling this move, but I didn't give a shit about morning breath. I wanted this woman exactly as she was. Scarred, bruised, exhausted, she'd never looked more beautiful. Probably because the damage wasn't from her standing there taking a beating like some goddamn punching bag. No, it was from her standing up to her ex and protecting her son like some avenging angel. Just thinking about what could have happened to them choked me up and made me desperate for her.

I tugged her shirt upward, and she broke off the kiss long enough for me to remove it. My hands immediately went to her exposed tits. They were perfection in my hands, and I squeezed and played with them until her nipples were hard peaks.

Rolling us over so I was on top, I removed her leggings and stood, stepping back to admire her body. She reached for the blanket, but I lunged, catching her wrists before she could cover up.

"Don't you dare hide yourself from me," I said. "If I'm yours, then you're mine, and I like to play with my toys. Last time we did this, it was all fast and furious like we were a couple of teenagers afraid of getting caught. This time, I want to worship your body like it deserves. Lie back and try to relax."

Surprisingly, she did as she was told, watching me as I stripped out of my clothes and settled myself between her legs at her feet. Grabbing her right leg in both of my hands, I kissed the inside of her ankle. With her hooded eyes fixed on me, she continued to watch as I worked my way up her calf, kissing every inch of her soft, pale skin. I found a ticklish spot behind her knee, and a spot on her inner thigh that made her break out in goosebumps. Her breathing took on an erratic edge as my lips approached her honeypot. I skimmed over the sensitive folds and dropped back down to repeat the process with her left leg. By the time I spread her lower lips and blew on her clit, she was panting and writhing beneath me.

"You like that?" I asked.

"God, yes."

She hadn't felt anything yet. "Good." I licked her from entrance to clit.

She about jumped off the bed. "Oh, oh, oh!"

Had that son-of-a-bitch never gone down on her before? I wanted to be pissed about his neglect, but honestly, I felt relieved. This could be something only we shared. I let the stubble of my jaw slide against her inner thigh, teasing. "Want me to do that again?"

"Yes." Her answer sounded a lot like a prayer. She was so needy and perfect.

"You sure?"

"Less talking. More—"

I licked her again.

"God, yes. More of that."

I got down to business, sucking, flicking, and swirling my tongue around her clit until she was fisting the sheets and speaking in tongues. I slid two fingers into her heat and took her over the edge. She tasted so damn sweet I made sure to lap up every bit of her honey before working my way north. I hadn't gotten nearly enough time with her incredible breasts, and they called to me, pleading for my attention. I showered them in kisses and nips while Tina ran her hand over my head and neck, and her gentle touch was surprisingly erotic. As I sucked one of her nipples into my mouth, she tightened her grip on my hair.

I liked that. I liked it a whole fucking lot.

I paid homage to her breasts until she was fully worked up again, and then I headed north, kissing my way up her breastbone to her neck. Covering that delicate spot behind her ear, licking her jaw line, letting her taste herself on my lips.

The heat between her legs called to my cock, promising a warm, safe haven. As I lined myself up at her entrance and slipped inside, it didn't disappoint. Wrapped in her silky-smooth heat, I hissed out a curse and started moving. She groaned against my lips.

"You feel heavenly, angel." I was trying to keep my pace slow, but my god, she was so damn tight. Gritting my teeth against the intense torture, I ground my hips against her and drove in deeper.

Holy shit, she felt even better when I was sober.

By the grace of God, I managed not to come until she did, but once she squeezed the life out of my cock and cried out my name, I was done for. Gripping her hips, I thrust myself deep, emptying everything I had inside of her. Collapsing, I tucked her against my side and pulled the blanket up to cover us.

"I love you, angel."

I could feel her smile against my chest. "I love you, too, Darius."

Feeling happier and more content than any fool had a right to, I drifted off to sleep.

EPILOGUE

Tina

KAOS WAS GETTING patched in. I didn't fully understand what that meant, but gathered it was an important step in his motorcycle club. He wanted me and Dylan there to celebrate with him. I was still kind of sketched out about the whole motorcycle club thing, but I trusted him. Besides, after all he'd done for us, supporting his promotion was the least we could do.

I couldn't remember the last time I'd worn makeup, but I was nervous and wanted to look my best. I concealed, powdered, lined my eyes, and then started swiping mascara onto my lashes. At the first swipe, the brush slipped out of my hand, bounced off the countertop and plopped right into the toilet.

Shocked, I took in the damage. Black streaks ran across the pale countertop, slashed the toilet seat, and marked up the bowl. Not to mention that my brand-new tube of mascara had been sacrificed to the potty gods. Disgusted with this turn of events, I put on a rubber glove, fished out the mascara, and tossed it into the trash.

Since only half of the lashes on one of my eyes had been coated, I used a makeup wipe to carefully remove my mascara. Peering into the mirror, I cursed my wimpy, insignificant lashes. It was Friday night, almost a month had passed since Matt's attack, and my bruises were long since gone. In fact, the whole ordeal was behind me. Between the video evidence that Morse had provided and Matt's coworkers that Link and Havoc had somehow persuaded to narc, the court had convicted Matt of numerous charges including attempted murder in the first degree, child endangerment, aggravated assault, and discharging a firearm in a public place. It would be at least thirty years before he even became eligible for parole.

My life was seriously looking up... despite the whole toilet mascara incident.

Cleaning up the rest of my mess, I gave myself one more once-over in the mirror and decided I looked presentable. Pushing away from the counter, I headed downstairs. It was time to go.

I'd left my hair down in soft curls that looked good, but probably wouldn't survive the ride. Kaos had bought me a special outfit for the occasion, and as I donned the distressed jeans, biker boots, and a tight Harley Davidson T-shirt and made my way down the stairs, I felt empowered by the hungry look he gave me.

"You look like a badass, Mom," Dylan said.

I probably should have called him out for swearing, but he was right. I did look like a badass. Besides, I'd gained a whole new appreciation for the more colorful adjectives of the English language, and I didn't want to discourage my son from using the most appropriate word for the occasion. At least, not at home. School was another issue, but we were working on that.

"Thanks," I said, hugging him as I took the black leather jacket that was dangling from Kaos's hand. His mouth was hanging open, so I closed it for him, patting his cheek to let him know he was a good boy.

Dylan laughed. I doubted he knew exactly what was going on between me and my man, but my observant boy had no trouble picking up on our moods. He knew enough to find my actions funny.

"Hot damn," Carisa said, looking me over as she came around the corner. "If I was into chicks, my cousin would have something to worry about."

Giving her my cheesiest grin, I said, "Why thank you. You look pretty amazing yourself."

She did, too. Carisa's outfit could also be described as badass biker chick, and her thick dark hair had been straightened to within an inch of its life. It looked sleek and shiny. War paint on, lips a perfect shade of candy apple red, I feared for the biker hearts she was guaranteed to break tonight.

"Thank you for stopping by to pick up Dylan," I told her.

She pulled me in for a hug only to dramatically push me away so she could look him over. "This handsome devil? Puh-lease. I should be thanking you. I've always wanted to be the lucky lady on the arm of the hottest guy in the place."

Dylan's cheeks turned crimson, and he let out an adorably shy giggle. "You look like a badass, too, Aunt Care."

I loved that he'd given her a nickname. The two of them had gotten ridiculously close over the past month, and I had no doubt Carisa would look after him like he was her own. Even in a biker club.

"Oh stop," she gestured for him to come to her. "You're already my favorite nephew. Just don't tell the others. We don't want to hurt their feelings." To me and Kaos, she added, "Ready to head out?"

"Let's do the damn thing," Kaos said, looking a little nervous, which was weird. I'd never really seen him nervous before.

We locked up. Carisa and Dylan climbed into her car while Kaos and I headed into the garage. He slid a helmet over my head, then popped open the visor to give me a kiss before putting on his own.

"I can't believe you talked me into this," I said.

"I only offered, angel. You could have ridden with Carisa and Dylan if you really wanted to."

He kicked a leg over his bike and took a seat, offering me his hand. I let him steady me as I slid in behind him and wrapped my arms around his midsection. He was right, of course. I'd chosen to ride with him because I wanted to. I'd met most of his blood brothers, but this was different. I was about to meet his club brothers... the brothers he'd chosen. Tonight was important to him, and I wanted us to arrive together. United.

Besides, he looked damn fine in his leathers, and I needed to make sure any club hussies that were hanging around knew he was mine. Leaning against him, I held on tight as he navigated the route. I didn't hate the ride. In fact, it was kind of exhilarating. I felt safe behind him, but also a little wild. We must have made quite the striking pair, because people stared as we rode by.

And for once, I didn't give a single fuck.

Kaos

When Tina and I pulled up to the fire station, Emily and Naomi were waiting for us.

"How are you doing?" Emily asked, focusing on Tina.

"Good." Tina's smile lit up her eyes and made my fucking heart soar. "Great, actually. I cannot thank you two enough."

Emily's gaze snagged mine and I gave her a nod, letting her know I hadn't changed my mind. "Good to hear," she said, patting Tina on the shoulder. "Naomi and I were hoping to steal you away for a few minutes. We have something we want to run by you."

"Is everything okay?" Tina asked, the pitch of her voice rising. "Matt's not—"

"No," Naomi said, cutting her off. "It's nothing bad. Just a little bit of paperwork."

Blowing out a relieved breath, Tina looked to me. "Do you mind?"

Ha! If only she knew. She would, soon enough. Stomach

clenching, I shook my head. "Not at all." Carisa pulled into the parking lot, and I waved at her. "I'll get those two troublemakers settled and meet you in the dining hall." Then remembering that she'd never been inside the club, I looked to the ladies.

"We'll show her where it is," Naomi assured me.

And then they were off. Feeling more nervous than a rookie with a pre-game puking problem, I turned and smiled at Dylan as he reached me. Over the five weeks that I'd known him, Dylan and I had come to an understanding. He didn't act up around me, and I treated him like the little man he was so desperate to be.

"You ready to head inside and see the place?" I asked.

He nodded, his gaze taking in the restored old building.

I watched him as we entered. Wide-eyed excitement lit up his face and had him firing off questions about the pool tables and dart boards. Promising him we'd get in at least a few games before we left, I kept to the edge of the room and tried not to catch anyone's eye. I needed to have a private chat with the kid before I'd be ready to introduce him. As I led him toward our destination, Carisa peeled off for the bar to get a drink.

Compared to the rest of the club, the dining hall was relatively quiet. Specks, our club treasurer, tried to wave me over, but I held up a finger, asking for a minute. His gaze snagged on Dylan, and he nodded. Leading the boy to the end of the table I sat, inviting him to do the same.

"You want anything?" I asked. "Water? Juice? Beer?"

He chuckled. "Sure, I'll take a beer."

Of course, he would. I stood and retrieved a root beer from the kitchen, setting it in front of him.

"This wasn't what I meant," he said, eyeing the can.

"Too bad. That's as good as you're gonna get."

Despite our goofing around, my nerves felt like exposed wires, all raw and vulnerable. I could go for a real beer myself, but I needed to be stone cold sober for this conversation.

"This is a cool place," Dylan said, looking around.

"I'm glad you like it. There'll be some kids here soon. Wasp's son, Trent, is about your age. Like his dad, he's a bit of a smartass. You'll like him."

Dylan grinned and set down his root beer. "Where's Mom?" he asked.

"Talking to Emily and Naomi again."

"Ah." He nodded. "You got stuck with babysitting duty again."

I stared at him, surprised. Without even knowing it, the kid had given me the perfect opening. "It's funny you should say that."

"Why?" he asked sounding confused.

"Because we both know I'm way too cool to be a babysitter."

Dylan laughed, and a little of the tension drained out of my shoulders.

"And..." I stared at him, wondering how to ask what I so desperately wanted to know.

Before I could even form the words, Tina came dashing into the room with a stack of papers in her hands. Emily and Naomi were hot on her heels. There were tears streaking down her face when she reached me. Waving the papers in the air, she said, "You... You want to adopt him?" Her voice cracked, and the hope and awe in her tone choked me up.

"What?" Dylan asked.

Tina must not have seen him sitting there, because her eyes widened, and her hand flew to her mouth.

"And, Dylan..." I started again, turning back to the boy and regaining his full attention. I was determined to finish my previous thought. Locking my eyes with his, I wanted him to see how very much I meant what I was about to say. "It's only called babysitting when the kid isn't yours. I want you to be my son. I want to adopt you. If you'll let me."

Eyebrows jumping almost to his hairline, he looked from me to his mom, and then back to me. "You... you want to adopt me?"

His bottom lip trembled. Tears welled in his eyes. It was all I could do to keep myself together. Swallowing back the ball of emotion that kept trying to lodge itself in my throat, I nodded. "Yes. With all of my heart, I want to be your dad." I let that sink in a moment, as he gaped at me, processing. "Emily assures me we can make that happen. But it's totally up to you." I glanced up. "And your mother, of course."

Tears continued to cascade down Tina's face, but she didn't move to wipe them away. "Whatever you want, baby," she told him as he looked to her. "This is your choice and there's no hurry. Take all the time you need to think about it."

When he met my gaze again, his watery eyes were running over, too. "I don't need to think about it." Giving me a lopsided smile, he visibly pulled himself together like the mature little man he was and nodded. "Yeah. Yes! Let's do this. I want you to be my dad."

Blinking back my own goddamn tears, I opened my arms. He flew into them, smacking his head into my chin.

"You know... this makes you way cooler," he said, squeezing me.

Laughing, I hugged the shit out of the little asshole.

My little asshole.

"You ready to go get patched in?" Link asked, breaking up our moment.

Releasing Dylan, I turned to nod at my president. "Sure am." Turning back around, I chucked Dylan under the chin. "Be good... Son."

He grinned at me. "I will... Dad."

That hit me right in the fucking feels. Taking one more moment to compose myself, I stood. Emily and Naomi had been joined by Carisa and several other women. I had no idea when they'd all come in, but there wasn't a dry eye among the bunch.

I didn't want to leave Tina and Dylan alone, but my cousin gave me a watery smile. "Go. I've got them."

I followed Link down the hall and into the chapel where we held the weekly meetings everyone called church. In a blur, the meeting was called to order and business was handled. Then Havoc called me up to the front and I was put on the spot.

Clapping me on the back, Link addressed the club. "I gotta be honest with you, brothers, I didn't know what the fuck to think about an NHL player turned soldier. Figured he'd be some kind of entitled little fucker."

Laughter and nods of agreement came from the group.

"But this man right here... he's solid. When the ladies needed him to step up and take in a single mother and her child, he didn't hesitate. Hell, he was the one who suggested it."

Feeling like a goddamn poser, I shook my head. If that was the reason I was finally getting patched in, Link was about to be sorely disappointed. "I didn't do it for Ladies First. I did it for Tina and Dylan."

Link nodded. "And when he fucked up, rather than make things worse, he called in and got orders."

"I wasn't tryin' to follow protocol," I said, coming clean. "I was looking for advice. I knew keeping her at my place would cross a line, and I didn't want do that shit. Matt had crossed enough lines, and... that wasn't what she needed."

"I know," Link said. "And that's why you're worthy to wear this patch. Stop being a dumbass and trying to talk us out of this. Look at this bunch, Kaos." His gesture encompassed the whole gathering. "A crew of fuck-ups with more issues than Sage can shake a stick at."

The club's shrink nodded in agreement.

"But they're good men who are just trying to help where they can. Just like you. Now shut your mouth and repeat after me." He walked me through the pledge, and once finished, he shook my hand. "Welcome, brother."

Everyone stood and repeated the greeting.

Within the span of a couple hours, I'd become a dad and gotten patched in. Feeling like the luckiest son-of-a-gun on the planet, I followed everyone out to the common area, where I found Carisa talking to Shari. Sneaking up on the two of them, I couldn't help but overhear their conversation.

"So, you just... sleep with all the bikers?" Carisa asked, her expression intrigued.

"Oh, honey, there's no sleeping involved. We fuck. But not all of them. I don't force myself on anyone. I have needs, some of them have needs... we provide a service for one another."

"And who do I talk to about signing up to be a... a club girl?" Carisa asked.

"A club whore," Shari corrected. "We wear that shit like a badge of honor."

That was about enough of that bullshit. "Nobody," I said, inserting myself into their conversation. "You're not becoming a club whore, Carisa."

She rolled her eyes and said, "We'll talk later, Shari."

"You most certainly will not," I roared. "I mean it, Care. Don't try me. I will tell your mom. Hell, I will announce it in my fucking Christmas cards so the entire family can kick your ass."

"Why, Kaos?" Shari asked, sounding like the very model of innocence. "Do you have a problem with consenting adults having sex? That's probably something you should talk to Sage about. Look, there he is now." She waved him over.

"Sage, huh?" Carisa said, checking him out. "I dunno, cuz. He's kinda hot."

I was about fifty percent sure they were fucking with me, but I glared at her anyway. "Bikers are off limits. They're my brothers now, and since you're my cousin, that's... that's incestuous."

"That's not really how that works." Carisa said, beaming a smile at Sage as he approached.

"Here, sugar, take this. You need to relax," Shari said, handing me a beer.

"Where's Tina and Dylan?" I asked, more than ready to get away from my hardheaded cousin.

She pointed to one of the furniture groupings. "Tina's over there talking to Elenore. Dylan's playing darts with a kid named Trent."

I spotted Dylan, who appeared to be having the time of his life, and then headed in Tina's direction. By the time I reached her, Rabbit appeared and was talking to Elenore. She said something, and he picked her up, carrying her away. I couldn't tell whether or not Elenore enjoyed it, but since Tina didn't interfere, I didn't either.

"What's all that about?" I asked gesturing after the couple.

"She's crazy. They're both crazy. I don't know. But I don't want to talk about them." Her face brightened as she stood. "How'd it go? You all patched up now?"

"Patched in," I corrected, pulling her against me for a kiss.

"Oh. Right. You all patched *in*?" she asked.

"Sure am." I turned, so she could see that I was no longer sporting a prospect patch on my bottom rocker. "You're lookin' at an official Dead President."

Her eyes lit up. "Impressive. Congratulations. By the way, I still can't believe what you're doing for Dylan. That was... that's really incredible."

My gaze cut to the dartboards where Dylan was throwing. "So is he."

Her eyes softened.

Squeezing her against me, I said, "So are you. You ready to talk about marriage yet?" I'd asked the question before, letting her know I was interested, but had no intention of rushing her.

She bit back a smile. "My divorce still isn't final."

"Counting down the days, angel."

Grabbing the sides of my cut, she grinned up at me. "Have I told you how hot you look in this thing?"

"I think you mean fuckin' hot," I corrected.

"Fuckin' smokin'," she said, one-upping me.

I loved her filthy mouth. "You know... there're rooms upstairs," I said, reaching around to give her ass a squeeze.

Her eyebrows rose. "There are?"

"Fuckin' rooms," I clarified, my grin widening.

"Just what kind of club did you bring me to, Kaos?"

I shrugged. "What can I say? Bikers are a horny lot."

"I see. You fit right in, don't you?" Her eyes narrowed to slits.

Sensing a trap, I answered honestly. "Only horny for you, angel."

Her smile held all kinds of approval. "Good answer."

"So, what do you say? Wanna sneak upstairs and have some fun?"

"What about Dylan?"

"Carisa'll keep an eye on him. And nobody here would let anything bad happen to him. He'll be fine," I answered confidently.

"I mean... I guess a quickie wouldn't hurt."

Wouldn't hurt? It would be amazing. I was already moving us toward the stairs. "Nobody'll even know we're gone." I squeezed her hand. "Come on. I hear club sex is the best, and I've been dying to get you here so we can try it."

"Well, when you put it like that..."

She let me lead her up the stairs. Going straight to the spare bedrooms, I found the first unoccupied one and pushed the door open, gesturing her forward. "After you, my dear."

"I had no idea bikers were such gentlemen," she said, brushing past me.

God, she had a nice ass. Without taking my gaze from her body, I locked the door behind us and kicked off my boots. "Trust me, angel, nothing I want to do to you right now is gentlemanly."

"Oh, really?" she said, yanking her shirt over her head. "Do tell. Or better yet, show me."

And that's exactly what I did, fully intending to keep showing her for the rest of our lives.

ALSO BY HARLEY STONE

Thank you so much for reading **Centering Kaos**. I hope you've enjoyed the journey.

Please take a moment to write a review. They only require twenty words and help me tremendously. I appreciate your support!

Also, be sure to check out my other books:

Link'd Up: Dead Presidents MC #1

Wreaking Havoc: Dead Presidents MC #2

Trapping Wasp: Dead Presidents MC #3

Landing Eagle: Dead Presidents MC #4

Tap'd Out: Dead Presidents MC #5

Breaking Spade: Dead Presidents MC #6

Betting on Stocks: Dead Presidents MC #7

Unleashing Hound: Dead Presidents MC #8

Taming Bull: Dead Presidents MC #9

Rescuing Mercy: Dead Presidents MC Spin-off

Until Selma: Dead Presidents MC Spin-off

Dom's Ascension: Mariani Crime Family #1

Making Angel: Mariani Crime Family #2

Breaking Bones: Mariani Crime Family #3

ABOUT THE AUTHOR

International bestselling author Harley Stone is a lover of animals, books, dark chocolate, and red wine. She's always up for a good adventure (real or fictional), and when she's not building imaginary worlds, she's dipping her toes into reality in southwest Washington with her husband and their boys.

ACKNOWLEDGMENTS

This book would have never become a reality without the help and support of so many people. Special thanks to my husband, Meltarrus, our boys, and all my friends and family for letting me off the hook when I daydreamed storyline and dialog during our conversations.

Huge thanks to the incredible Gail Goldie, who saw this first and saved the rest of the world from having to read most of my mistakes. Also, thanks to my fabulous friend Nicole Phoenix for her content edits, suggestions, and encouragement. Thank you, beta and ARC readers for your edits, support, and love.

And, thank you, reader, for embarking on this journey with me!

Printed in Great Britain
by Amazon